BENOTRIPIA

KEYS TO THE DREAM WORLD

MCKENZIE WAGNER

Enjoy the adventures!

[signature]

SWEETWATER
BOOKS

An Imprint of Cedar Fort, Inc.
Springville, Utah

Cover and inside illustrations by Rachel Sharp

This is a work of fiction. The characters, names, incidents, places, and dialogue are products of the author's imagination and are not to be construed as real.
The views expressed within this work are the sole responsibility of the author and do not necessarily reflect the position of Cedar Fort, Inc., or any other entity.

ISBN 13: 978-1-4621-1435-1

Published by Sweetwater Books, an imprint of Cedar Fort, Inc.
2373 W. 700 S., Springville, UT 84663
Distributed by Cedar Fort, Inc., www.cedarfort.com

LIBRARY OF CONGRESS CATALOGING-IN-PUBLICATION DATA

Wagner, Mckenzie, 2000- author.
  Keys to the dream world / McKenzie Wagner.
    pages cm. -- (Benotripia ; [3])
  Summary: Working tirelessly to protect their island, Roseabelle, Jessicana, and Astro find themselves under attack, discovering that in order to save Benotripia, they must find the passage to the Dream World--and destroy it.
  ISBN 978-1-4621-1435-1 (perfect : alk. paper)
  1. Children's writings, American. [1. Friendship--Fiction. 2. Dreams--Fiction. 3. Magic--Fiction. 4. Fantasy. 5. Children's writings.] I. Title.
  PZ7.W1245Ke 2014
  [Fic]--dc23
                                            2014016889

Cover design by Kristen Reeves
Cover design © 2014 Lyle Mortimer
Edited and typeset by Melissa J. Caldwell

Printed in the United States of America

10 9 8 7 6 5 4 3 2 1

For Ty,
the most creative Benotripian of them all.

Contents

Contents

CHAPTER 1

Astro

WHEN ASTRO WOKE UP THAT MORNING, HE had planned on doing a lot of things, but falling from the sky was not one of them.

Stretching and yawning, he rolled out of bed, already dressed in rumpled jeans and a black T-shirt. He then crossed over to the window and threw aside the heavy midnight-black drapes so sunlight could pour into the room. He slid open the heavy glass pane and welcomed the fresh air that drifted inside. Slinging his leg over the windowsill, Astro boosted himself onto the ledge.

There. That was better. A lot better. Astro lived inside a gray stone tower that dated back to who knows when. His father had inherited it from his father, who inherited from his father, and so on. It had belonged to the Jagged-Bolt family for generations. They had never moved, probably because (aside from the arsenal in the very top room) there wasn't a smidge of metal to be found in the tower. They'd discovered that the neighbors didn't appreciate a lot of bright flashing, which was what usually resulted when any of them touched metal, because most Jagged-Bolt family members, including Astro, were born with the power to shoot lightning bolts from their fingertips.

He gazed at the beach in the far distance—one benefit of living in a tower was the fantastic view. Astro spotted many Benotripians already gathering to resume building the defenses. Ever since the Darvonians—their heartless enemies who lived on another island—had snuck onto Benotripia in hopes of stealing the Stones of Horsh, Danette (the leader of Benotripia) had decided they needed more security. She had put together a plan for the Benotripians to build watchtowers. If the Darvonians attacked, they would be ready. Danette had personally marked certain places on the beach's outer edges where the ground was hard enough to build a foundation. The defense towers looked pretty good to Astro; they were towering structures with endless barracks of magical tools and weapons stocked inside.

You would think that after obtaining the most powerful artifacts in history, people would pay attention to you, maybe let you in on what they were planning. Dastrock (Roseabelle's uncle) and Danette often had secret meetings—and it drove Astro crazy just thinking about it. Did they know something about the Darvonians' plans? Roseabelle, Danette's daughter and Astro's best friend, had told him she didn't know anything either. Six weeks previous, Astro had gone to her house, but Dastrock and Danette had shooed him away, purposely avoiding his questions and telling him to go to find Roseabelle outside.

Shortly thereafter, Dastrock and Danette left Benotripia on a sea vessel, and Astro hadn't seen them for five weeks. They had traveled to the outer edges of Darvonia to monitor their enemy. Astro reckoned Danette just wanted to be extra cautious.

His fingertips crackled with electricity, and Astro sighed with relief. After his Stone had made the Darvonians and their mysterious shadow horses disappear using its own ability, his hands no longer shook with pain when he used his power. When the Darvonians brought the shadow horses to the island, they radiated so much electricity, it had overloaded

Astro and caused immense pain. But that didn't mean the shadow horses weren't out there—he still needed to be cautious. Speaking of the Stones of Horsh . . . Astro reached into his pocket to run his fingers over the smooth, hard texture of the red Stone. Horsh, a Darvonian who had joined forces with the Benotripians, had created the Stones and applied magical abilities to them. Astro still didn't understand why he had created them—that was another mystery still to solve.

Astro had assumed that Dastrock would know a way to destroy the Stones, but Roseabelle's uncle had just shaken his head. "I wish I could," he had said. "They are a true danger to the Benotripians. But they are protected by various enchantments and can't be destroyed by steel, fire, Dragocone Rays, not even the other Stones. For now, you will have to keep them safe and hidden away. Never reveal them in the open." Dastrock wanted to destroy the Stones, because although they had extraordinary powers, if the Darvonians got hold of them, all would be lost. It was better they didn't exist at all, for the safety of Benotripia. Astro also wondered why in the world Dastrock would trust him, Roseabelle, and Jessicana with the Stones. "If the Darvonians do attack, the first place they'll choose to search for the Stones would be the leaders of the Benotripia. Believe me, they'll be safer in your hands."

It was tempting to show off the Stone to others, but Astro obeyed Dastrock anyway.

Swinging his legs over the windowsill, Astro curled his fingers into a tight fist. It was strange how much Benotripia had changed since the Darvonians had invaded the island. The schools were temporarily closed because most adults needed to help construct the defenses and every child needed to be practicing their powers.

Astro thought back to the last time he'd spoken with Roseabelle and Jessicana, just a few days ago. "I'm a little worried," Roseabelle had said. *Of course she's worried*, Astro thought. *The Darvonians will stop at nothing to conquer Benotripia.*

"Worried about what?" he'd asked her.

"Sheklyth," was her reply. Astro grimaced at the name of Roseabelle's former trainer. Sheklyth had betrayed them all, revealing to Roseabelle when they had gone to rescue Danette that Sheklyth wasn't just a Darvonian, but the heir to the Darvonian throne.

"Why? We all saw Astro's Stone make her vanish," Jessicana said.

"I know, but . . . I can't shake the feeling that she's not gone."

Maybe it was crazy, maybe it was absurd, but Astro had a strange feeling that Roseabelle was right.

For some reason, Astro sensed that Sheklyth was alive. He didn't know how or why, but he just did. Astro's gaze locked onto something in the corner of his room, tucked behind a shelf. The files they had retrieved from Darvonia, the ones that had gotten them into the castle, still lay there. He, Jessicana, and Roseabelle had figured out they'd been talking about Metamordia—that was the secret thing the Darvonians had been discussing. What would Metamordia be like anyway? Tropical, like Benotripia? Rocky, like Darvonia?

As he gazed out on the landscape of the tropical island, immersed in his thoughts, Astro suddenly saw a silver projectile hurtling toward him out of the corner of his eye. It happened so fast that Astro barely had time to duck forward. It was a weapon!

Although he avoided it, the act of ducking caused Astro to lose his balance. Before he knew what was happening, he dropped like a stone, the air ripping past his face, his arms flailing wildly. In his panic, silver lightning shot from his fingertips, peppering the ground below.

The wind whistled obnoxiously in his ears, and Astro tried to grasp anything he could. At one point, he grazed the rough-hewn stone of the tower, but he was hurtling toward the earth so fast, it was impossible to hold on.

The only thing he could think of as the [ground] rushed up to meet him was: "AHHHHHH[H"

Desperately, he shot a large lightning bolt at the ground to boost him up and slow his fall, but it merely created a smoking black hole in the dirt instead. Just as he was about to smash against the ground, something jerked him to a stop, suspending his body horizontally two inches above the earth.

"Wha-what?" he said shakily. Suddenly the hold on his body gave way, and he plopped down on the ground.

"Astro!" said a familiar voice, and he turned to see a wide-eyed and terrified Jessicana running toward him, blonde hair flowing around her shoulders. As Astro moved to get up, he noticed a rope around his waist, tied to a metal hook. Jessicana wore the Grapplegore, a bulky ring on her finger with a glistening green gem. Her trainer, Asteran, had given the ring to her. Every time Jessicana pressed on the green gem, two ropes swung out, one to latch on to something and another to attack any intruders from below. Normally, Jessicana used it for swinging from vine to vine. "Are you all right?" she asked, helping Astro to his feet.

"Yeah," he said, rubbing off the shock of plummeting eighty feet. "What happened?"

"I-I was walking to go to Roseabelle's house, when

I decided to come here to invite you, and I sort of saw you falling from the sky," she stammered.

The realization struck him. "You saved me," he said.

"I'm glad you're all right. Um, by the way, why were you falling from the sky?" Jessicana's eyebrows crinkled a bit.

"I saw something coming toward me," Astro explained. "Looked like a weapon ready to slice off my head! And since I was sitting on the windowsill, I tumbled out."

"A weapon?" Jessicana asked, her voice shaking a bit. "Are you sure you weren't imagining things?"

"I'm sure!" Astro said. But it had all happened so fast, he wondered if he really was just daydreaming. Maybe the silver projectile flying toward him hadn't been a weapon—maybe it was just a bird. But he could've sworn it wasn't normal.

Jessicana gestured to the smoking black hole in the ground. "Goodness, your lightning sure got out of hand!"

Astro walked over to the hole. "There goes Mom's garden." As he peered over the edge, a flash of color caught his eye. What was that? All sorts of surprises today! Kneeling down he heard Jessicana walk up beside him. Was that . . . some sort of musty white contrasting against the black dirt?

Reaching his hand into the pit, his fingers grasped a rough trutan, a type of parchment in Benotripia, and he yanked it out, clearing away the dust and shaking off the layers of dirt. "Where'd you find that?" Jessicana asked as Astro held it up against the light.

"Just right here," he said. *What is this? Some sort of outdated scroll?* he thought.

Jessicana pointed to a spot on it in the top left corner. Astro realized it was the symbol of Horsh— three Stones balanced on a person, one in the left hand, one in the right, and one balanced on the head.

"We should show this to Roseabelle," Jessicana said excitedly. She blew away some of the dust. "I can't make out most of the words but the three of us together just might." She and Astro stood together, and he shook his head, almost in amusement.

It was funny how he could discover things completely by accident.

As the two walked away, a pair of large golden eyes peered out from underneath a bush, intensely focused on the young Benotripians. In a moment, they sunk back into the shadows.

Jessicana and Astro hadn't noticed anyone watching them.

CHAPTER 2
Dream World Scroll

A S SOON AS ASTRO SLIPPED THE DUSTY
parchment inside his pocket, Jessicana suggested they head over to Roseabelle's house.
It'd been a while since she'd seen her friends, and it would be nice to talk with them.

As they trudged through the sand, Jessicana saw a cluster of bizarre animals race past them—probably a shapeshifting Benotripian family. Danette and Dastrock had left orders to build defenses and be prepared, and the Benotripians had definitely taken them seriously. In the distance, Jessicana could see Benotripians hard at work, structuring the large stone towers that would be used to fight the Darvonians.

But personally, Jessicana didn't believe the Darvonians would suddenly storm the island. They were much more clever than that.

She and Astro finally arrived at Roseabelle's home, and Jessicana's heart leaped to see her friend already sitting on the porch, feet dangling in front of the rope ladder. Roseabelle's house was positioned in a large tree. On Roseabelle's arm was a lightly speckled brown-and-white mottel, a special type of bird that could send messages. It kept repeating the same message in Danette's voice. "Roseabelle, check the defenses and make sure the Benotripians are doing their jobs. Dastrock and I are well, and we are keeping constant watch on the Darvonians, making sure they aren't sending any war fleets to attack the island. Be safe. I love you."

"Roseabelle!" Astro called from the ground, and they saw their friend beam at them.

"Hey!" Roseabelle greeted them. "Danette just sent me a message."

"Isn't that the first one in five weeks?" Jessicana asked.

Roseabelle nodded. "Yes, but it's a long way for a mottel to travel." She signaled the mottel to remain on the porch while Jessicana ascended the rope ladder. Astro quickly followed.

"My mother wants to me to check the defenses on the beach. You want to come along?" Roseabelle asked.

"Sure," Astro said. He peered into the distance. "It looks like they're doing their jobs, that's for sure." Jessicana had to agree. The stone towers grew higher every day.

Roseabelle laughed. "I know, but I should probably check them up close anyway. Besides, it's a good excuse to talk with you two." The three friends descended the rope ladder, the mottel balanced on Roseabelle's bare arm.

They trekked to the beach, sand coating their sandals. Jessicana took in the breathtaking view of the crystal blue waters washing up on the golden shores. And then she saw the defense towers before them.

Benotripians were racing to and fro from the massive stone structures, carrying supplies and weapons. The structures seemed to tower over the tiny figures of the three friends. Jessicana could see spiraling staircases when she peered closer. Many Benotripians were using their powers to improve the construction.

"Looks like they're doing what they're supposed to," Roseabelle said, nodding her approval. She gave a report to the mottel and it flew away, darting over the deep ocean, soaring high among the clouds. "I gave him a few hours to rest because he had a long journey. So what's going on with your lives?"

"I nearly died today," Astro said cheerfully.

Roseabelle's eyes nearly bugged out of her head. "What?"

"Long story," Jessicana intervened. "But look what we found." Astro dug out the wadded up piece of dusty trutan from his pocket, and Roseabelle unraveled it, scouring it quickly.

"It has Horsh's symbol on it!" she exclaimed. "Where did you find this?"

"I—" Astro was about to continue but halted in mid-speech. Jessicana felt chills run up her spine. Was it just her or did she feel eyes boring into the back of her head?

Suddenly, her face turned ashen as a silver blur flew toward her friends. "Get down!" she yelled as she plowed into Roseabelle and Astro. She knocked them over and looked up just as a Thepgile Disc soared over their heads. A noisy clatter echoed behind them as the circular weapon with the cord attached dropped to the ground.

"Who threw that?" Astro said, glancing over his shoulder.

"No time to talk! Let's get back to your house!" Jessicana insisted. Something really odd was going on. First, Astro was shot at and now all three of them were being targeted! Her breath caught in her throat. Was it possible? . . . No, she didn't want to think about that now.

Without another word, the three of them raced back to Roseabelle's home, not bothering to search for the weapon someone had hurled at them. They needed to hide now! Jessicana's pulse raced and she searched the sky behind them as they ran, but she spotted no one—and, thankfully, nothing else flying toward them. The Benotripians working on the towers had been so focused on their tasks, it was unlikely that they noticed the attack. And with so many people milling about, Jessicana hadn't noticed any Darvonian dark cloaks. She shivered. Maybe someone had been hiding.

They ran up the rope ladder and threw themselves into Roseabelle's home, panting for breath. "Well, I guess someone really wants us dead," Astro said, wheezing.

"Close the windows," Roseabelle ordered. "Lock the door. What's going on? What's on that parchment?"

"We don't know," Jessicana said, scrambling to clasp the lock on Roseabelle's front door as Astro pulled out the trutan. "We can't decipher it. It's too faded."

Roseabelle and Jessicana both peered at the document, scrutinizing the faded writing. Suddenly, Roseabelle's eyes lit up. "I have an idea!"

Roseabelle raced upstairs and Astro and Jessicana quickly followed. They burst into Danette's study. "My mother uses a tool for these sort of things," Roseabelle said excitedly. Digging in Danette's two desk drawers, she soon brought out a tiny silver instrument.

It had a small head with a glassy surface and small teeth ruts. The sheen of the metal was distorted and coated with a thin layer of dust. Roseabelle pressed it down on the trutan, the ruts clearing away some of the deep dust, revealing words positioned on the trutan. "This is an Embele," Roseabelle said. "My mother created them because when people sent her documents and letters, sometimes they got dirty. Probably a prank or something." She proudly held the Embele in front of the trutan. "There."

Astro whistled. All of the grime had been scratched off and Jessicana could now decipher the words. Roseabelle handed it to her. "You want to read it aloud?"

Jessicana shrugged. "Sure." She narrowed her eyes a little bit, trying to understand the miniscule writing. She gasped. "It talks about the Dream World!"

Astro raised his eyebrows. "What does it say?"

Jessicana turned back to the paper and began to read. "'The Dream World is a real, physical place,'" she began. "'In my studies, I have learned that the ancient Benotripians used their powers to create the Dream World—an invisible passageway between the three islands of Benotripia, Metamordia, and Darvonia. With their powers, the Benotripians turned the Dream World invisible and levitated it, sustaining it to remain in the air. They also gave it the gift of sonic speed, so that anyone inside it can travel at the speed of wind. For centuries, the inhabitants of the islands used the Dream World to travel between the islands, both physically and with their minds. There was, for a time, peace among the nations.

"'However, years later, the Darvonians betrayed our trust. They attempted to take over the Dream World. Doing so would have allowed them to travel to Benotripia and Metamordia instantaneously with numerous armies and creatures. They failed only because I locked the doorway with the Stones before they could gain access. I must now hide the Stones, before they find the doorway again. The doorway is—'" Jessicana stopped and frowned deeply. "The ink is smudged over the rest of it." She found her friends gaping at her as they comprehended the message.

She remembered how Roseabelle had entered the

Dream World with her mind when she had touched the feather Jessicana's trainer Asteran had dropped— it was crazy to think that the Dream World was an actual place. "This document might be phony," Astro said. "It could've been planted by the Darvonians."

Jessicana shook her head. "No, I don't think so. Look." She pointed to the worn writing and the symbol of Horsh. "This lettering is too ancient to be made from the Darvonians just recently. And look at the emblem of Horsh—it's exactly the same as the one behind the waterfall."

Her friends nodded. "It seems as though Horsh really did write this," Roseabelle muttered to herself. "But we can't be sure. It could still be a trick."

"The Stones of Horsh were a myth and they turned out to be real," Astro pointed out.

"Yes, but this is a little too coincidental," Roseabelle said. Jessicana had to agree. How did a page of Horsh's diary get so near Astro's home?

"Still, it's all we have. We might as well rely on it," Jessicana said, then glanced out the window. "I need to get home."

"Same," Astro said. Roseabelle tucked the trutan in her pocket.

"We'll figure it out," she promised as Jessicana and Astro went to the door.

"We better race home before anything else falls from the sky and tries to kill us," Astro said, assuming a runner's stance. Jessicana nearly laughed at the ridiculous sight.

"Yeah, that'd probably be best." Then they flung open Roseabelle's front door and charged toward their homes, feet flying and hearts racing.

CHAPTER 3

Walk in the Night

Hours later, Roseabelle sat up in her bedroom, reclining on her bed. Liquid moonlight streamed through her window, illuminating the room. She recalled that Danette had made her promise to not leave Benotripia unless there was a dire emergency.

But she wanted to help Danette! And even though Danette and Dastrock had gone to monitor the Darvonians, Roseabelle was sure danger was lurking around in Benotripia. The only problem was she didn't know what. All she could come up with was that it had something to do with the enemy island.

"Only leave Benotripia if there is an emergency,"

Roseabelle whispered, wondering what counted as an emergency. Probably a known ambush from the Darvonians or black ships in the distance. Definitely not because Astro fell from his tower—Jessicana had finally told her the story.

The trutan lay on her dresser, blending in so that she couldn't even see it from her angle. Would she need to use it sometime soon? Part of her almost hoped so.

She decided to go on a quick walk to clear her head. There was no way she would get back to sleep with all these thoughts plaguing her mind. Roseabelle quietly unlatched the window and slid onto her mango tree, grasping the thick branches and leaping down onto the soft, grainy sand. Striding along a path, she breathed in the cool, fresh air. A light breeze slipped past her face, making her red hair flutter.

Cottages, tree houses, schools, libraries, and other buildings dotted the landscape around her, and she weaved between them and eventually spotted Jessicana's tree home. Crickets chirped and diverse flowers and plants bobbed on their stems from the flower beds.

The looming shapes of the defense towers caught her eye and Roseabelle's interest sprung. She had never been up close to the defenses; she had just watched the Benotripian workers from afar except for her quick visit earlier that day. Roseabelle made her way down to the beach and put her hand against the smooth, polished stone, amazed that the Benotripians could build a structure as large and complicated as this.

Danette had never set any rules about touching or going inside the defenses, she reasoned—though the Benotripian people wouldn't appreciate a mere child investigating one. Still, Roseabelle was incredibly curious. What exactly was inside? She knew there was an enormous stock of weapons and supplies, but were there any plans, any clues? Deciding to be quick, Roseabelle searched for an entrance and eventually found a stone handle.

She pulled with all of her weight, but the handle wouldn't budge. *Oh, well.* When Danette returned, Roseabelle would ask to explore the towers. She plopped down on the white sand and gazed out into the ocean. She could see a tiny dot in the distance, but maybe it was just her imagination. After all, it was dark. She squinted to see the getaway boats docked at the side of the beach, carrying supplies.

A deep low growl broke the silence of the moment and Roseabelle whirled around, eyes scanning the area frantically. What was that?

It couldn't be a wild animal—those creatures preferred the Benotripian jungles, not the beaches! Besides, the beach was empty except for mounds of sand, some bushes lining the far sides, and, of course, the three defense towers within her reach. Beyond those, open paths stretched back to the city of Royalton.

No animals appeared.

"Hello?" Roseabelle called softly, rubbing her head. Maybe she was hallucinating. After all, it was pitch black, almost midnight. She should head back home.

But as she headed toward a path, the growl once again resounded in her ears, and Roseabelle flinched, quickly pivoting in the direction the sound had come from. The bushes rustled quietly and Roseabelle backed up, groping for anything that she could use as a weapon or at least something to protect herself with. What could it be, some sort of Darvonian animal? Or was it a person?

Roseabelle took a couple of steps back, her eyes wide. A smooth shape glided out of the bushes and a pair of golden eyes stared and then narrowed at her.

In the darkness, Roseabelle couldn't make out the creature and, as another low growl emitted from the figure, she backed up a few more steps. She kept her eyes trained on the creature, waiting for the beast to follow her, but the golden eyes didn't move. "What are you?" she whispered, thinking about her power for sensing animal's emotions. If only she could get close enough to touch it. But what if it was a Darvonian animal that would rip her to shreds? She had never heard of a golden-eyed Benotripian beast before.

The darkness completely immersed the creature. Even in the moonlight, Roseabelle could only make out its faint figure. The eyes stared back at her without the slightest hint of aggression. Tentatively, she took a step forward. "Easy," she whispered as the low growl came again.

Roseabelle froze, afraid it was going to pounce. Instead, the creature moved slowly. Roseabelle watched in awe as the majestic creature suddenly came into her view. She awkwardly stumbled back a few paces, mouth gaping open at the sight before her.

The large creature had mottled black-and-red fur, a slim body, and four paws the size of dinner plates, covered in white feathers. Its head was roundish with a horned snout and a streak of white feathers on its smooth forehead. Roseabelle noted that its body structure reminded her of a wild cat's.

Those enormous golden eyes still stared at her as the creature slowly approached.

Roseabelle didn't know whether to run or to stay put. She had never seen this animal before— it wasn't Benotripian! But she had never heard of animals like these on Darvonia either. It growled again, and she caught a glimpse of its brilliant array of white teeth.

She sensed something else in its eyes, however, that contrasted with the growl—a hint of peace. Its muscles, rippling deep under its fur, were loose, and its expression was almost playful.

Roseabelle inhaled a deep breath and out-stretched her trembling fingers to the side of the animal's head, wondering why she was trusting it so much not to attack her. Maybe she was crazy, but she had a feeling that, inside, this wasn't just an ordinary animal.

As soon as her fingers touched the sleek fur, Roseabelle concentrated and slowly closed her eyes. Instantly she felt a rush of overwhelming surprise that she'd found something—found what? Then, as Roseabelle dug deep into the layers of emotions, she began to feel like she was floating in air. The creature was perfectly at peace and full of tranquility. She sensed no hostility or harmful feelings inside, not even gnawing hunger. Honestly, it was weird. There was also a burst of intelligence, and she had the feeling that the creature knew everything that was going on around him.

But the strangest thing was when Roseabelle realized that the energy of these feelings were focused on her.

Roseabelle snapped open her eyes to find the pleading golden orbs staring right back at her.

But what if this was a trap? Despite the peace she'd felt from the animal, Roseabelle couldn't shake her nagging worry. She chanced a quick look over her shoulder. Everyone in the nearby houses was still asleep.

Jessicana. Jessicana would know! She loved animals and she had read probably thousands of books on them. Roseabelle looked in the direction of Jessicana's home. Her friend would know where this animal had come from. But it was still very early, and Mrs. Wingling probably wouldn't appreciate her daughter's best friend and a strange animal coming to their house in the middle of the night to talk. Roseabelle turned back to the strange creature.

"I'll come back for you in the morning," she said, kneeling on the ground and rubbing its head. Roseabelle stayed extremely still as the animal whimpered.

"I'm sorry, but you have to stay out here for the

night," Roseabelle whispered. "I'll come right back here in the morning, all right?"

The creature just stared at her, but as she stroked the side of his head, he purred softly. As Roseabelle straightened up, the creature, swift as the shadows, darted away into the night. There was a distinct rustle of bushes and then Roseabelle was alone.

CHAPTER 4

Moonstar

ASTRO SPRINTED ALONG THE PATH TO ROSEA-belle's house, anxious to talk to his friends again. At the crack of dawn he'd been awake, and after meandering around the tower for a little while, he'd decided to get dressed and head over to see Jessicana and Roseabelle again. As he ran, the red Stone thumped in his pocket, reminding him that it was still there.

Around him people were walking, flying, and even burrowing into the earth, traveling around the island. He accidentally bumped into a group of women near a cluster of trees who were practicing using their powers by transforming into various animals. Astro muttered an apology and weaved through the trees, wishing he, like Jessicana, could turn into a parrot and fly for once. As a pair of bird-shaped Benotripians almost collided over his head, however, he decided that maybe it was okay just running.

Surprisingly, when he got to Roseabelle's house, both she and Jessicana were already on the front porch. "We have to show you something," Jessicana said as he rushed up to them.

"What is it?" Astro asked, the wheels in his head already turning. But a breathless Roseabelle just motioned for him to follow them.

"I went walking last night," she said. "And found something crazy."

Astro had seen a lot of crazy things in his life—probably more than he needed to. But what was Roseabelle talking about? They sprinted across the paths to the beach, keeping away from the Benotripian workers. The girls led him to a more secluded spot, where the sand met the cerulean waves and the outer edges of the leafy jungle. "What is it?" he asked.

"Um, please just don't freak out," Jessicana said. "He's friendly."

"Who's friendly?" Astro asked, but the answer came straightaway when a deep, chilling growl rattled his spine. He whirled around to see a large cat with black and red fur pacing toward him. He jumped slightly at the sight of it. "Guys, I'm not really interested in becoming lunch right now." He backed away slowly, staring in wonder at the animal's golden orbs.

"It's fine," Roseabelle said. "I've read his emotions, and he won't attack you."

Astro accepted her words but didn't break eye contact with the creature. "Wait, so he just came up to you?"

Jessicana answered the question. "I think he's been looking for her all along. They must have formed a special animal bond. I've read about those. Anyway, he's not from Darvonia or Benotripia."

"He has to be from Metamordia then," Astro said. There was no way this creature had just appeared from thin air.

"That's what I was thinking," Roseabelle said and knelt next to the creature. Astro flinched but the animal only purred in response.

"Why's he so feathery?"

"No idea," Jessicana said. "But what's even more curious is how he got here."

"Maybe a stowaway of some kind," Astro suggested, and Roseabelle's eyes went wide.

"That could be it," she mused. "But a stowaway on whose boat?"

Astro thought about the weapons flying at him. Was it even possible? Had Darvonians really traveled to the island again? But no sightings had been reported. What about Metamordians? But there had been no contact with that island for years. Why would they suddenly show up? He had the urge to say something but resisted. Right now they had a mystery at hand to solve. "So why did we meet him here?" Astro asked gesturing to the animal. "Someone might see us. Should we go to your yard, Jessicana?"

"He led us here," Jessicana said, and to prove her point, the animal nudged his head on the soft sand. She walked over to Roseabelle, who had been casually folding and unfolding the parchment in her hand. Both of them stared at the parchment. "I wonder if this really is authentic . . ."

But Astro's eyes had veered from the girls and he now stared, transfixed, at the creature. Was it just his imagination or was the animal jerking his head toward something? The large cat purred and pawed through the sand, and Astro's eyes shot up. Getting down on his knees, he dug through the wet sand, getting his elbows deep in the grungy mess. "Something down here, boy?" he asked, feeling a little silly. Talking to a weird creature that was from a different island? Yep, he was going crazy.

But as he dug, Astro felt his arms abruptly enter a hollow space. Looking down at the sand, he realized he had unearthed a small pocket of air in the beach. "Roseabelle, Jessicana!" he yelped. The creature stared at him, its golden eyes almost holding a playful smirk. He could almost imagine it saying, "I told you so."

The girls scuttled over to them and Jessicana grinned. She knelt beside Astro and yanked out something from the dirt, a silvery object. Roseabelle immediately handed her the Embele and Jessicana furiously scraped at it, revealing a spyglass.

"Where did this come from?" Roseabelle asked. Astro gazed at the object, his curious nature perking up. Almost in response, the creature dug into the pit. When he raised his head, something silver hung from his mouth and he dropped it on the beach. Astro lifted it to his face, realizing it was a tag of some sort fashioned out of grimy silver. The worn letters displayed "Moonstar."

Astro glanced at the creature. "Moonstar," he whispered. "So that's your name." Moonstar rubbed up against his leg, purring quietly.

Jessicana suddenly stumbled back, holding the spyglass to her eyes. "No way," she murmured.

"What is it?" Astro asked. He felt as though an extravagant mystery was being unfolded before them, and his fingers tingled with excitement. He had to remind himself to keep his power under control as silver lightning flashed. He quickly stuffed his hands into his pockets.

Jessicana held out the spyglass to Roseabelle, who accepted it. She peered into it and her jaw went slack. "You're not going to believe this, Astro," she said, handing it to him.

He raised the instrument to one eye and stepped back in disbelief. Astro had expected to see only a short distance, but instead he saw a close-up view of Darvonia. The rocky dark landscape brought back bad memories and Astro yanked it away from his face. "No ordinary spyglass, for sure," he said.

"It's not even extended!" Roseabelle exclaimed.

"Must be a magical relic," Jessicana mused.

Astro once again raised the spyglass to his eyes, extending the silver attachments and increasing the view. He tilted it skyward—and saw something floating midair: an shimmery, airborne tube, clear as though it were made of glass. Astro couldn't see inside it, though. He pulled out the other increments in the spyglass, getting an even better view. The tube stretched as wide as the sky. "What is that?" he asked.

"What's what?" Jessicana asked.

"There's some sort of tube," Astro said. He

retracted the increments, staring at the sandy Benotripian beach, but the glass floating structure was still there.

He handed it to Roseabelle, and she twisted it around. Astro noticed that when he was staring at the air above the ocean with just his eyes, he saw nothing. But with the spyglass, something was definitely there. "I think this spyglass can see through enchantments," Roseabelle said, concentrating hard on where Astro was pointing. "Wait a second," she said. "Astro, hand me Horsh's papers."

He picked up the trutan from the ground and handed it over to Roseabelle.

"I think this really is genuine!" she exclaimed. "You're not going to believe me but Horsh says the Dream World is a real place, but invisible, right? Well, I think I might be staring right at it."

"No way," Astro whispered. Could that glassy tube actually be the Dream World?

Roseabelle handed the spyglass to Jessicana. "Think about it. What else could the spyglass be? It lets you see faraway distances. Why couldn't it see magical properties of things as well?"

Astro noted that Roseabelle was getting excited, the prospect of discovering something new gleaming in her eyes.

Jessicana set down the spyglass. "Um, guys, I think there's something else you should see."

"What is it?" Roseabelle asked, and Jessicana let her peer into the miniature telescope.

"I think your family might be in trouble, Roseabelle," Jessicana said, her usual perky bounce gone.

When Roseabelle pulled away from the spyglass, Astro saw that she looked troubled. "Let me see!" he said and peeked through the spyglass.

He skimmed across the dark waters, catching a glimpse of the clear glass tube. Astro could now see the outer edges of the dark island and his interest piqued when he saw a fleet of black ships moving. His pulse raced—they were Darvonian ships. Weren't Danette and Dastrock supposed to be monitoring them?

He swiveled the spyglass to see the distinct forms of the Benotripian ships not too far away. But they were sailing right toward the Darvonians, as though they hadn't even seen the dark ships.

Each of the friends peeked through the spyglass once again. "I don't get it," Roseabelle said, pacing back and forth, running a hand through her bright red hair. "Don't they see them coming?"

"Maybe not," Jessicana said. "It's possible the Darvonians have some protective fog around them."

"So Danette and Dastrock think they have the upper hand," Astro said, piecing it together.

"But in actuality," Jessicana said, exchanging a look with Astro, "they're the ones being trapped."

"I think you're right, Roseabelle," Astro said. "The Darvonians might be using an enchanted fog to conceal themselves and we can see it because of the spyglass."

It happened as quick as a flash and Astro didn't even have time to react. A black arrow, appearing from nowhere, sailed toward his midsection. He cringed, waiting for the blow.

But it never happened. Glancing down, he saw the arrow embedded in his pocket—it had struck the glistening red Stone inside. Roseabelle and Jessicana looked at the trees in horror, and Moonstar perked up, alert.

And then time seemed to slow down for Astro as the dark figures of Darvonians appeared in the trees—their black soulless eyes staring straight at him.

This time Astro knew exactly what they wanted.

The trutan had to be genuine—they had seen the actual Dream World with the spyglass and now Darvonians were after the Stones, the Keys to the Dream World.

CHAPTER 5

Setting Sail

FOR A FEW SECONDS, THERE WAS ONLY SILENCE. It seemed as if the Darvonians were scrutinizing them, wondering why the three friends hadn't moved yet. They were still frozen, immersed in shock.

"Run!" Astro shouted, and the trio tore out of the beach, kicking up sand in their wake. Jessicana nearly slipped and Roseabelle quickly steadied her. Running right along the water, Astro felt his fingertips already crackling in alarm, his heart pounding like a bass drum. How had the Darvonians snuck up on them like that?

"Where are we going? There has to be somewhere we can hide!" Jessicana yelled.

In the lead, Roseabelle shook her head, panting. "I have a better idea."

They raced in front of the Benotripian defense towers. Glancing up, Astro saw the citizens looking torn—they could obviously see the Darvonians right there, but there were also three Benotripian kids that they couldn't risk hitting with Flame-hurler Missiles.

Astro chanced a look behind him. The Darvonians were chasing after them like a hungry mob, and Astro saw them release a cloud of black arrows. Knowing that he and his friends couldn't survive such an attack, he quickly grabbed Roseabelle and Jessicana. The three of them instinctively ducked, sprawling on the sand as the arrows flew right past them.

Rising to her feet, Jessicana shouted, "Go, go, go!" They resumed sprinting across the beach. Moonstar bounded behind them, seemingly comprehending the danger they were in.

The Darvonians were right on their tail, and Astro wondered where Roseabelle was headed. But then he saw it—she was racing right for the emergency getaway boats!

"You're not really—" he started but his worst fears were confirmed just seconds later.

"Yes, I am!" Roseabelle shouted back and tore toward the docks. Astro's legs were getting tired but he urged himself to go on. He turned in time to see the Darvonians firing arrows again. He stretched his fingers out, an array of silver lightning shooting rapidly at the Darvonians, peppering them with deadly energy.

Some of his bolts exploded as they collided with a storm of arrows; others knocked the Darvonians off their feet. But to Astro's surprise, the rest of the Darvonians kept coming.

"Get away from here!" Roseabelle shouted at Astro and Jessicana. "I'm Shadow Tumbling back to the house to get the trutan and some weapons. The Darvonians will follow you. Above all else, keep the Stones safe." Shadow Tumbling was one of Roseabelle's many powers—it allowed her to travel through shadows. Astro opened his mouth to argue, but Jessicana beat him to it.

"What about the people?" Jessicana asked.

"I'll make sure they follow us and leave the Benotripians alone. Hurry, they're gaining on us! I'll be right back." Roseabelle dove into the shadow of a large tree, then closed her eyes and disappeared, spinning into the depths of darkness.

The other two reached the docks, and Jessicana hurriedly untethered a particular boat, her hands working at the knots at an unbelievable pace. Astro leaped into the spacious wooden boat, and Moonstar quickly followed after him.

The Darvonians came closer. Out of the corner of his eye, he saw a couple of the Darvonians turning to face the Benotripian people, weapons in their hands. Quick as a flash, Astro leaned out the side of the boat and aimed. An eruption of silver bolts sprang from his fingertips, slicing through the air. The lightning hit the attacking Darvonians and they fell to the ground, unconscious. The lightning attack delayed the other Darvonians who were attempting to revive their fallen comrades.

Jessicana finished separating the boat from the dock and stepped inside the boat, casting a nervous glance at the Darvonians closing in on them.

"I'll paddle, you shoot!" Jessicana instructed, her hands shaking. As the Darvonians raced up the dock, Astro shot a firm wall of lightning at them, his arms trembling. The force was almost too much for him, and he was tiring quickly.

With the Darvonians only slightly delayed, Jessicana and Astro steered the boat away from the docks, paddling furiously. But before they knew it, the Darvonians had cut the main rope and compressed themselves in the boats, eyes glinting, power hungry for the Stones. Roseabelle had been right. They were so driven to retrieve the Stones, they were leaving the island just to follow Jessicana and Astro.

Jessicana paddled furiously, and Astro quickly drove his oar deep into the water—but they were moving too slowly. The Darvonians were speeding toward them now. At the front of the boat, five archers drew back their thick bows, deadly black arrows nocked in place. If those arrows were loosed, Astro knew he and Jessicana wouldn't have a hope—the Darvonians were well known for their deadly aim.

Acting on an impulse, Astro compressed his hands together and formed a crackling ball of electricity, which glinted silver and blue on the waves. Jessicana's eyes widened, but she continued paddling as Astro gritted his teeth, forcing all of his energy into his hands, and raised the charge above his head.

Then, with a mighty yell, he hurled the crackling ball of light at the enemy. Both he and Jessicana ducked for cover. A bright flash followed by a sizzling crack illuminated the water. Cautiously, Astro quickly peered over the rim of the boat. Half of the boats were in splinters, and the Darvonians that had previously occupied them were swimming frantically to the other watercrafts, boosting themselves into them. Astro had created a gaping hole in one of the boats. He grinned—only a couple boats remained perfectly untouched. And the boats that had shattered had lost all their weapons and supplies.

"Nice job," Jessicana said, grinning. "That was like a thunderstorm next to the ground!"

"Maybe that's because it was," Astro said teasingly, and Jessicana rolled her eyes.

"Whatever." They high-fived. Suddenly Roseabelle appeared beside them in the shadow of the stern, red-faced and sweaty, the trutan tucked under one arm and a bulging sack clasped in her hand.

"You nearly gave me a heart attack!" Jessicana breathed.

Astro tried to calm his racing pulse. He hoped that the sack was full of food and weapons.

Roseabelle blushed. "Sorry. I got everything we need."

"Roseabelle, where are we going?" Astro asked. Moonstar purred in agreement, and all three of them jumped. They'd completely forgotten he was there.

"To find my father, Magford," Roseabelle said. "With the Darvonian attack, I'm absolutely sure that Horsh really did write this and that the Dream World is a real place. We've got no one. Danette and Dastrock are too far away to reach. The least we can do for them is send them a mottel. Magford can tell us where the Dream World is."

As the boat pulled away from Benotripia, Jessicana asked, "But what if this a trap from the Darvonians? They could be misleading us."

"Right now, I suspect the Darvonians just want the Stones. They aren't focused on tricking us. Because they know, once they have the Keys, it doesn't matter anymore. If they can travel to Benotripia within seconds, they could surprise attack us with armies, creatures of every kind . . . they can take over the island without even trying. We can't let them open the Dream World and take control." Roseabelle spoke firmly, and Astro had a feeling she was right.

The Darvonians didn't care about tricking them anymore. Or did they? Well, whatever they were thinking, Roseabelle had a good point. Astro smiled at Roseabelle's confidence, although he didn't feel confident, if his racing pulse was any indication. "Then Metamordia, here we come!"

CHAPTER 6
Sea Ambush

LEANING AGAINST THE SIDE OF THE BOAT, Jessicana whistled sharply, and the splitting noise echoed across the waves, reverberating all the way to the beach. She was signaling one of her mottels. Jessicana then joined her friends at the stern. She took a bit of time to study the boat they were in.

It was a large boat, fashioned of thick wood and outlined with metal. As Jessicana peered over the side, she could see cerulean waves brushing against the hull. Complete with a billowing white sail, the boat had control levers to steer it, and a sturdy masthead and a trapdoor leading into a cabin belowdecks.

Jessicana decided that this was the best way to travel to Metamordia.

Astro was currently steering the boat, and Roseabelle was in back, watching the Darvonians with the spyglass. "They're quick on our tail," she reported. "Not within weapon range, though. We need to keep out of their reach, because they're not afraid to destroy our ship. Remember, they just want the Stones."

Tingles ran down Jessicana's arms. "Roseabelle, what weapons did you bring?" she asked, and Roseabelle motioned to the trapdoor.

"Astro, can you handle the upper deck for a bit?" Roseabelle asked. "I'm going to grab our supplies."

"Sure," he responded. "But hurry."

Jessicana followed Roseabelle as they descended the rope ladder. Moonstar was in the corner, sprawled out on the wood, fast asleep. Roseabelle led Jessicana to the sack and yanked out their old backpacks. She tossed one to Jessicana.

Jessicana unzipped it to find a javelin, a bow and quiver of arrows, a coil of rope, a collection of snacks, and two water bottles. When she dug in farther, she also discovered a Spidegar and her mini potion kit. The Spidegar had multiple threads attached to tiny blades. When someone held onto one end and threw the other part of it, all of the threads lashed out at once to create a deadly weapon.

"Wow, you grabbed all that in a few seconds," Jessicana said in admiration. "How did you do it?"

Roseabelle shook her head. "I've had these packs in my bedroom for months. Danette had me store them there in case of an emergency." She picked up the other two packs and started up the rope ladder.

Jessicana followed her. Once she reached the top deck, she spotted one of her mother's mottels perched on top of the stern. Astro was looking questionably at it. "Uh, Jessicana, you're the bird expert. Do something about this thing," he said

She rolled her eyes and stepped forward. "I summoned it here. It's to carry a message to Danette and Dastrock." She clucked her tongue, and the mottel instantly leaped onto her forearm, its floppy toes curling around it. Its deep brown eyes stared into hers.

Roseabelle shot her a grateful smile, then bent low next to the mottel. "Mom, this is Roseabelle. Darvonians are surrounding you and Dastrock; we're going after Dad. It's a long story. Just get off that ship at all costs. I love you." Roseabelle paused, and Jessicana figured she was finished. She nodded at the mottel and it flapped its wings and flew away into the sky. She watched as it rose among the clouds and then soared away from sight.

As her face split into a grin, Jessicana turned to Roseabelle. "Well, that worked out!" But her friend just stared into space. "You all right, Roseabelle?"

She nodded. "I'm fine."

Astro rolled his eyes. "You're such a bad liar, Roseabelle."

Roseabelle seemed to snap back to reality and offered him a lopsided grin. "Uh-huh. Keep steering the boat or we'll crash into Blackwater Sea. And that's not recommended."

"Are we sure that Metamordia is only accessible across Blackwater Sea?" Jessicana pointed out. They didn't have a map and that worried her a bit.

"No, I'm not sure, but all we can do is hope for the best. I'll look for any detours." Roseabelle then scooped up the spyglass to her face, pressing her eye against it once more. Jessicana peered back, but she couldn't see the Darvonians anywhere. With luck, they would stay that way.

Astro seemed to know what he was doing, but Jessicana felt inclined to do something on the ship. "I'll steer if you want," she offered.

He shook his head. "Nah, I'm good. But we do need a good scout."

"Of course you do," Jessicana said teasingly, then began transforming into a parrot. A tingle shot up her spine as vivid feathers grew on her arms, sprouting into various bright colors. Her aqua blue eyes started moving from the front of her face to the sides. A folding sensation raced through her as she shrunk and developed a more squat, roundish shape. Whenever she performed her power, Jessicana felt like her transformation took a while, but it actually passed in a matter of seconds.

Squawking, she rose to the air, and the boat shrunk into a tiny dot. Jessicana swooped back to survey the miniscule fleet of Darvonian boats. All they were doing was collecting supplies and weapons. Her friends were in the clear, at least for now.

She settled into the rhythmic wave of gliding through the air.

FIVE DAYS SHOT BY, AND ROSEABELLE HONESTLY didn't remember most of it.

She and Astro took alternate turns manning the controls and keeping a lookout for the Darvonian boats overtaking them. So far, so good. Jessicana patrolled the skies and always alerted them if their enemies were drawing long-range weapons, in which case they sped ahead.

As Roseabelle stood on the deck, veering the boat left and taking a swig of water from her canteen, Jessicana suddenly crumpled on the deck beside her. "Jessicana!" she exclaimed and knelt down to her friend. "You all right?"

She quickly sat straight up. "Sorry, I crashed. Was flying too fast." Roseabelle's friend spoke in hurried gulps of air. "The Darvonians—they're too close. They've developed a . . . new form . . . of the Dragocone Ray. Looks like a harpoon. Going to . . . reel us in."

Roseabelle's eyes shot wide open, and she glanced up at the sky. It was evening, and the sun reflected bright pinks and yellows across the glinting water as it slowly sunk behind the horizon. Astro was asleep belowdecks. "Wake Astro up," she whispered. "We might have a fight on our hands."

Jessicana nodded swiftly and disappeared, darting down the trapdoor. Roseabelle knelt down and unzipped her pack in a flurried frenzy. *This isn't good*, she thought. She patted her tunic pocket, feeling the heavy white Stone inside. They had to keep the artifacts safe.

Just then, Astro appeared through the trapdoor, grumbling. "What is it?" he muttered. Jessicana emerged right behind him.

"The Darvonians are about to attack!" Jessicana

said. "And the winds are fast enough to give us an extra burst of speed." That really woke Astro up. Roseabelle turned away from her friends and rummaged through her pack, finding silk gloves, a Dragocone Ray, a sword, a couple of throwing daggers, and a Flame-hurler, complete with six packages of ammo.

"Astro, you steer! Use your lightning against anyone who appears in front of the boat. Jessicana, you stand on the boat with your bow. I'll go in the water."

Astro did a double take. "What? You can't breathe that long underwater!"

Roseabelle and Jessicana both stared at him.

"Dolphin girl, remember?" Roseabelle resisted a grin. She was lucky her friends could lighten the mood in situations like these. She knew that if the Darvonians overtook their ship, they could drown and the Stones would be easy for their taking.

"You're going to attack their ship, right up close?" Jessicana asked as Roseabelle kicked off her shoes. "But you can't carry weapons as a dolphin!"

Roseabelle's idea seemed to fade right before her eyes. Jessicana was right. How could she have forgotten that? Suddenly, she lit up. "You have rope in your pack! Maybe I could tie my sword around my waist with it. Make sure to give some slack too. I'm a lot thicker as a dolphin." Jessicana nodded and quickly obliged, digging in her pack. Astro seized the spyglass and raised it to his eyes.

"Jessicana was right. They do have some sort of harpoon. They're lining it up against the boat," he reported. Roseabelle's blood ran ice cold. They couldn't let the Darvonians get the Stones.

Roseabelle grabbed her sword and sheathed it, then accepted the rope from Jessicana. This had to work. If she attacked the Darvonians from behind, maybe they wouldn't get the chance to harpoon their boat. Even now, without the spyglass, she could see their group of boats speeding toward them.

"Hurry!" Astro urged.

Jessicana placed the sword against Roseabelle's back, then began to wrap the rope around her waist. Roseabelle held the sword in place as it was tethered around her. When the sword was finally bound in place with quite a bit of slack rope around her midsection, Roseabelle flashed a quick smile in her friends' direction.

"Shoot your bow toward the Darvonians," she told Jessicana. "And, Astro, you know what to do." Then before either of them could speak up, Roseabelle turned and dived into the water, picturing herself blending in with the smooth cerulean waves and her legs morphing into a tail.

Just as the cool water touched her face, Roseabelle felt her skin become more leathery and her feet bind together. She could suddenly breathe in the water and felt the sword's heavy weight on her back. Sound became distinctively muted, and, sure enough, she knew she had turned into a dolphin.

Diving deep, Roseabelle flicked her tail, heading toward the enemy's boats. She headed straight toward them, slightly held back by the weapon she was carrying. She allowed the slack to take place and let the sword carry its own weight in the water, drifting above her, held by the ropes around her midsection.

Bubbles swished up from her mouth. Speeding up by flicking her tail faster, Roseabelle was suddenly aware of the wildlife around her. A few bright green fish swam right past her, but she focused on pushing ahead. Above, she could distantly hear an array of frantic shouts, and she hoped desperately that her friends were all right.

Tilting her head, she could see several dark shapes on the surface and immediately recognized them as the Darvonian boats. Propelling herself even quicker, Roseabelle veered around them and came up from behind, momentarily surfacing. She closed her eyes and imagined her legs dividing and her lungs once again breathing in oxygen.

Her wish was granted as the feeling returned to her legs, and when Roseabelle surfaced, her drenched red hair hung around her shoulders and the sword hung from her slim figure.

And she was right behind the cloaked figures of the Darvonians.

CHAPTER 7

Spires of Rock

BREATHING IN COOL FRESH AIR AND TREADING water as silently as she could, Roseabelle counted five boats in all, packed with cloaked Darvonians. She pushed through the water and swam right beside the closest one. The boats were slowing down so the Darvonians could solidify their aim. Placing her hands on the side of the boat, she boosted herself up. Luckily, the Darvonians in the boats were at the stern, focused on the fight ahead, and not in the back where she was.

Jessicana had been right—there were glowing objects that looked like Dragocone Rays, but they were shaped like harpoons instead. Wearing silk gloves, one of the cloaked figures suddenly turned around to grab one. Roseabelle ducked, hanging on to the side of the boat.

Counting silently in her head, she figured it was safe to come up.

"Ready?" said a gruff voice.

Roseabelle poked her head above the boat and reached behind to untie the sword from her body. Her fingers slowly worked on the knots, and she willed them to move faster. One Darvonian stood and suddenly shouted, "NOW!" A dozen brilliantly glowing harpoons flew across the skies, straight toward Jessicana and Astro.

Roseabelle saw most of them erupt in a cloud of crackling silver lightning before they could reach her friends, and she resisted letting out a cheer. But then she spotted a spreading hole in the hull of their boat. One of the harpoons had struck it.

The Darvonians began to throw another array of harpoons, but Roseabelle still hadn't freed her sword yet! She gritted her teeth. *Just a few more knots*, she thought.

As the Darvonians prepared to attack Jessicana and Astro again, Roseabelle spotted a barrel of water right behind them. Clenching her teeth, she focused on it, and her telekinesis took over. The wooden container rose in the air, liquid sloshing over the lid and spilling onto the deck.

At the sudden noise, the Darvonians whirled around, but before they could reach her, Roseabelle quickly tilted her head and the heavy barrel plowed into them. The Darvonians were knocked over and doused with gallons and gallons of water.

Her sword suddenly became free, and Roseabelle quickly unsheathed it. One of the Darvonians in another boat leveled an arrow at her, and she twitched, focused. As he released the arrow, Roseabelle caused it to fly backward, knocking him overboard.

More Darvonians lunged for her. She thrust the hilt of the sword against the helmet of the man closest to her, and he quickly toppled overboard. One enemy seized her ankle, and Roseabelle tripped. The Darvonians rushed to seize her.

Thinking quickly, Roseabelle leaned to the side of the boat with the most Darvonians. The weight of so many people capsized the boat, flipping it over—and the Darvonians' harpoons with it.

A wave of water washed over Roseabelle's head, and she fought to hold her breath. In the chaos, she slipped out from underneath the overturned boat, escaping the Darvonians' clutches. She cast her eyes toward the dark underside of the boat carrying her friends. She could see the glimmering shapes of the Dragocone Ray harpoons that had missed, sinking to the bottom of the ocean.

The Darvonians were still distracted—Roseabelle noticed their waterlogged cloaks were weighing them down. Seizing her opportunity, Roseabelle managed to kick upward, her head breaking through the surface. A shout rang in her ears: "There she is!"

In shock, Roseabelle noticed a new group of Darvonians leaning over the side of their boats, all eyes focused on her. The other boats hurled more harpoons at Jessicana and Astro. Roseabelle realized her sword was gone and she only had her powers to rely on.

One of the cloaked figures found a Dragocone harpoon and quickly aimed it at Roseabelle. Quick as a flash, she closed her eyes and transformed into a dolphin. She dived just as the deadly weapon sank into the waves after her.

Underwater, Roseabelle flicked her tail and came up underneath the boats, ramming into the hull. She rammed it again and again. The boat jostled violently, and sure enough, as she gave it one last try, the boat capsized, spilling a dozen Darvonians and their weapons into the sea.

Roseabelle knew there were three more boats to go. She realized that if she got rid of their weapons instead of the boats, she and her friends would be safe. For now, anyway. Morphing back into a human, Roseabelle resurfaced from behind the Darvonians and saw the cloaked figures searching everywhere for her.

"There!" one yelled. Roseabelle lunged for the boat, spotting the Dragocone Rays inside. A humming filled Roseabelle's ears and using all of her remaining strength, she levitated the deathly weapons. Before the Darvonians could grab them, Roseabelle jerked her head to the left and they dropped into the watery abyss.

But when she looked up, she saw that one Darvonian still had a Ray harpoon. The enemy's eyes narrowed and drawing back, he hurled the weapon straight at Roseabelle. Her eyes grew wide and she sank into the water, the missile singeing the top of her red hair.

Treading water, Roseabelle rose to the surface, but instead of hearing frantic shouts directed toward her, the sound of pouring water reached her ears. She glanced to the left and saw that the harpoon the Darvonian had thrown had impaled the other boat beside it. Water was gushing inside it, and the Darvonians were hurriedly finding a way to escape. Some jumped out and swam to the other boats. She stifled a laugh—the Darvonians had just sunk one of their own crafts!

Diving, Roseabelle closed her eyes and made the transformation once again into a graceful dolphin. It was time to go back to her own boat—she hoped it was still floating.

JESSICANA WORKED FURIOUSLY TO FIX THE GAPING hole in the boat. Moonstar was still miraculously asleep, and Jessicana was plugging the gap with a large piece of thin slated stone that had been stored along with crates and emergency food and water.

She sealed the stone in place with some old chewy wraptook, a kind of bread that stuck like glue. Adding some wadded up cloth to plug in the holes, Jessicana managed to fix the hole, and the water stopped leaking in. Glancing around in dismay, she realized at least four inches of water had seeped in. Still, it was better than the entire boat sinking—and it certainly didn't seem to be bothering the slumbering Moonstar.

Astro poked his head down through the trapdoor. "Roseabelle's back!" he called. Jessicana scurried up the rope ladder to see Roseabelle, drenched, boosting herself back into the boat. Her friend was weak and her limbs were shaking. Astro had to pull her the rest of the way into the boat.

"I saw what happened," he said, grinning despite

his exhausted state. "You took down three boats! And all of the harpoons! Nice work, Roseabelle."

"Thanks," she said. "Did you patch up the hole?"

Jessicana wiped the beads of sweat off her forehead. "Yeah. That hole was sure stubborn." In truth, she was just glad to see Roseabelle alive. "We had better steer ahead to get away from those Darvonians. Astro, you should've shot a few Flame-hurlers at them."

"I know," he said. "But Roseabelle had it covered." Astro reached inside his pocket. "It might be a little helpful to use the St—" He stopped abruptly and lifted the Stone to eye-level; Jessicana's eyes widened in surprise. She could see that the once-brilliant light that gleamed in the Stone was gone. The dull red jewel seemed to be lifeless.

Roseabelle noticed as well, and she and Jessicana withdrew their Stones from their pockets. The shimmer, the light glowing from within, had vanished.

"Do they still work?" Jessicana asked, her voice penetrating the shocked silence. She waved her Stone toward Roseabelle, picturing a flower appearing in her red hair. But nothing happened.

Astro tried his as well. "The power's been sucked out of them," he said. "At least, that's what it looks like."

Roseabelle surveyed the Stones while Jessicana studied her own. Had she done something wrong?

Maybe the Darvonians had enchanted it. No, that wasn't right. The Stones were extremely powerful artifacts; no one could just tamper with them like that.

"They were glowing when we left," Roseabelle said. "So we can't despair. My father will know what's going on. We just have to focus on protecting them." Jessicana glanced up at the sky, realizing how dark it was. The sparkling stars contrasted deeply against the pitch black of the night.

"Can I go back to sleep now?" Astro grumbled, and Jessicana and Roseabelle both grinned at each other.

"Knock yourself out," Jessicana responded. Astro flung open the trapdoor, then scrambled down the ladder. "Speaking of sleeping, what's wrong with Moonstar?" It was strange—Moonstar had been asleep the entire voyage! Even though Jessicana didn't know anything about this species, she really was worried about him sleeping for so long.

Roseabelle scowled. "He hasn't eaten or drunk anything, has he?"

Jessicana shook her head. "It's odd for an animal. Usually all they want to do is eat." Being part animal, she should know.

Jessicana picked up the spyglass and resumed her original position. She stared at the waves with their hypnotic rhythm. Gazing into the distance, she saw that the two black Darvonian boats bobbed on the water, and she was pleased to see that they were going just as slow as her ship was.

Suddenly Roseabelle spoke, nearly making Jessicana jump. "Jessicana," she said, speaking softly. "Do you think my mother's going to be all right?" Jessicana instantly felt guilty. Here she was just minding her own business, while Roseabelle was thinking about her mother. Jessicana was impressed by how well her friend hid her feelings.

Jessicana walked up to Roseabelle and squeezed her hand. "I don't know, Roseabelle. But as long as we're doing our best, Danette will be just fine."

Now she had to convince herself to believe it.

Two more days passed on the ocean, and the three friends took turns alternating between resting, steering, and keeping watch for any signs of danger as they steered toward Metamordia. The ocean was relatively calm, and Astro was glad they didn't have to pass through Blackwater Sea. After all, his definition of fun was not sailing through deadly black waters where only death and danger awaited.

Only hours earlier, Jessicana had spotted with their spyglass the fight between Danette's ships and the sneaky Darvonian fleets. There had been cannons and bright flashes of Dragocone Rays, but the fleets had retreated further into the distance and she couldn't see them anymore.

Astro glanced toward the trapdoor. He was amazed that during this whole time Moonstar had been asleep. Lucky animal. While everyone else was fighting, the creature was taking a nice long nap.

Right now, Astro was at the steering wheel, clenching it tight, peering straight ahead. He had counted that a week had now passed and his stomach wobbled a bit. Both of his friends were extremely lucky—Jessicana could get off the boat at any time and fly in the clouds for a few minutes, and Roseabelle could transform into a dolphin and freely swim. Astro didn't have the freedom to get off the boat at all, and as a result, seasickness was starting to bother him.

"See anything?" he asked Roseabelle, who was standing near the boat's railings.

"I can't tell," Roseabelle mused. "There's a lot of mist up ahead but we've traveled so far that Metamordia's bound to be close."

Astro turned back to steering as tiny crystal waves lapped at the hull. He honestly didn't know if they could handle being out here for much longer. They were already running low on food. What if they had completely missed Metamordia? No, that wasn't possible—the spyglass could see through enchantments.

"Wait!" Roseabelle exclaimed, lengthening the spyglass suddenly.

"What is it?" he asked.

"Nothing good," she said and held the instrument toward him. Astro snatched it and held it to his eye, looking for anything strange. All he could see was open water and an enormous mass of white fog. Squinting, he noted that the only thing beyond the fog was an endless sea of blue.

"I don't see anything," he said.

Roseabelle took him by the shoulders and jerked him to the right.

"Look closer," she insisted.

Astro did, and just as he was about to put the spyglass down, a blur of darkness flashed past his vision. "What was that?" he whispered to himself. The boat suddenly shuddered, and Astro nearly dropped the spyglass.

Jessicana came up through the trapdoor, rubbing her eyes. "Something wrong?" she asked sleepily.

A horrible grinding split the air and Astro winced. Yikes! What was that? He gripped onto the side of the boat with one hand and peeped through the spyglass with the other. His mouth agape, he saw what lay ahead of the boat.

Dark twisted rock spires and clumps of enormous boulders rose majestically out of the sea like giants. Astro wondered if the boat was skidding on pieces of rock right at that moment. He realized with a start that the spyglass was no longer extended at all—the spires were right in front of their eyes. They had been too busy looking way ahead to see what was right in front of them.

"We've got trouble," Roseabelle said.

Astro put down the spyglass and saw their boat barely miss a towering black rock spire.

"Where'd Metamordia go?" he asked urgently.

"It has to be beyond this rock," Jessicana said. "This is another Darvonian trick. Remember last time? We had to make it through that cloud of fog in Blackwater Sea to get to Darvonia. There's always an obstacle to pass. This one just happens to be crazy-looking rocks jutting out of the ocean. The Darvonians don't want anyone finding their way to the third island, that's for sure." Astro couldn't see very well through the mist that was sticking to the sides of the boat—the rocks seemed to pop out of nowhere.

"We have to steer out of here!" Astro exclaimed, reaching for the controls. There was no way they'd survive going through there. Their boat would be demolished and they would be stranded.

"Wait," Jessicana said, taking the controls first. "The Darvonians designed it like this. If we veer off course, we'll have to go through a different obstacle. We'll never get to Metamordia. Blackwater Sea is full of too many surprises. We have to go straight through."

Astro stared. Jessicana was absolutely right. "Kinetle's cloak, sometimes the Darvonians are so clever it hurts," he muttered.

"We need some sort of protection for the boat," Roseabelle said and instantly dashed off.

"Where are you going?" Jessicana called, but Roseabelle was already below deck. The boat tipped slightly as the hull scraped against a rough piece of submerged rock. Astro grabbed onto the stern, dropping the spyglass. It rolled around on the deck.

"Watch out!" he yelled at Jessicana. Yanking her down, they watched as a spire of rock, jutting out from a monstrous boulder, appeared where her head had just been.

"Thanks," she said, giving him a quick smile. Roseabelle came racing back .

"Get down," Astro said, worried that more rock spires might appear. "What's your plan, Roseabelle?" It wouldn't be long before the jagged rocks sliced through the wood of the boat like putty. If Roseabelle didn't have a plan, it seemed like they were done for.

Roseabelle was holding the trutan in her hands along with a bottle of ink and a quill. As she was running, some of her ink had spilled on the wood, staining the deck purple. Astro noticed her hands were shaking uncontrollably.

"What should we draw?" Jessicana asked.

"Wooden planks," Roseabelle said. "And tools. We're going to need to patch up any holes these rocks might make."

"Can't any of your powers help with the Stones?" Astro asked. Although the trutan was better than nothing, it wasn't as fast as the Stones of Horsh. Eventually, these rocks would get the better of them and their boat would sink.

Roseabelle pondered the question for a moment while Jessicana began drawing frantically. "Telekinesis," she suddenly burst. "Of course! It'll take a lot of effort though. I might be able to move the rocks away from the boat with my mind. Astro, you man the sides of the boat and chop off any rocks that come near us with a Dragocone Ray. Jessicana, you keep drawing." Roseabelle took her position at the front of the boat and Astro dashed below deck to find a Dragocone Ray. Avoiding the puddles of water, all he could think was, *This had better work.*

CHAPTER 8

Metamordia

ROSEABELLE STOOD AT THE STERN, FOCUSING hard and warming up her mind. Beforehand, she already knew that this was going to wear her out, maybe to the point of total exhaustion. But it didn't matter. Her friends' lives were in jeopardy, and this was the only way they would make it to Metamordia.

This was the only way they would make it *alive*.

Shadowy shapes leered at them from above, jagged rock spirals sticking out from different angles. As a cluster of enormous boulders appeared, Roseabelle swerved the boat to avoid them. Glancing up ahead, she could see piles of loose black rock jutting out of the surface.

Clenching her teeth and clearing her mind, Roseabelle focused on the rocks, blotting out every other sound, every other movement. She made a motion with her arms, and the cluster of rocks wobbled slightly. "Come on," she muttered, thinking of her father on the other side of this stone graveyard. "He's just past this point. Come on, Roseabelle, you can do this. For him. For them."

Grunting, body pumping with adrenaline, Roseabelle lifted four of the rocks mere inches in the air. They skimmed the water and plopped into a different part of the ocean, where they disappeared below the surface. Face red and breathing heavily, Roseabelle focused on the other clusters of rocks that lay in their path. As they approached a second pile, she panicked, realizing she couldn't do it. Her mind was sore from the exhaustion of the previous lift.

"Brace yourselves!" she yelled as the boat headed dead on toward the rocks. Just as they were going to hit, Astro ran up behind her. With a quick downward swish of his Dragocone Ray, the rocks split into numerous pieces and sank to the sea floor. "Thanks," she said.

"Don't thank me yet," he said with a worried grin. At that moment, the ship slid into a cloud of white fog, and Astro and Roseabelle looked at each other nervously.

"The spyglass can see through this fog right?" Astro asked.

Roseabelle nodded. "Give me the Ray. Use your lightning but don't hit the water. With the combined Telekinesis and weapon, I should be able to move the rocks out of the way in time. We can't afford another blow."

Astro handed Roseabelle his Ray and slid off his silk gloves just as another rock spire dug into the ship's wood. He could hear Jessicana's triumphant shout as she finished patching the previous hole—then her groan as she realized there was another one.

With the Dragocone Ray gleaming brilliantly, Roseabelle could see relatively well through the fog, and with the spyglass, so could Astro. A jagged rock spire jutted from the side, and she hurriedly slashed through it, the rock splashing through the water. Astro's lightning severed the boulders so quickly that soon a path appeared, free of the rocky dangers. Astro cheered in delight as the fog and debris ahead of them cleared to reveal a pristine ocean free of obstacles. He exchanged a high-five with Roseabelle.

And then all the glee drained from their faces. Up ahead, as though in slow motion, a towering mass of smooth black obsidian popped up from the waters. Roseabelle's eyes widened, and she hit the deck.

Acting on instinct, Astro grabbed the Dragocone Ray and flung it at the spire. As the Ray came into contact with the rock, a burst of fiery energy emitted, sparks flying in every direction. The rock was severed from its position, cut jaggedly and glowing bright red. The spire sank into the sea, causing monstrous waves to wash over them.

Several moments later, Roseabelle looked up—coughing and sputtering from being completely doused. Her heart was beating faster than usual. "Nice thinking," she said to Astro. He was kneeling beside her, equally soaked.

Jessicana came running up, panting. "I finished," she said. "But that was *not* easy. Below deck is pretty much ruined. We still have our supplies—" She was cut off as the three were almost blinded by white light.

Blinking and shielding their faces, they realized the fog had cleared and sunlight had poured into their view. But that wasn't all they saw. Jessicana leaped in her excitement and gripped the wooden railing of the boat, and Roseabelle let out a huge sigh. "Amazing," she gasped. Beside her, Astro's eyes nearly popped out of his skull.

The island before them was lush, with green grass growing everywhere. A glistening crystal waterfall gushed from a smooth brown cliff, and rolling hills were complemented by trees that grew rich green leaves. It was nothing like Benotripia, yet it shared the same exotic beauty.

"Metamordia," Roseabelle gasped.

Beside her, Astro took in the amazing sight, then frowned, running a hand through his spiky black hair. "There are no people. Isn't that a little strange?" Jessicana shrugged. From behind them, Moonstar suddenly bounded up and out of the open trapdoor. "So now he wakes up," Astro said, groaning playfully and the animal obediently slunk next to Roseabelle, purring softly. She patted the animal's head and bent down next to him, her mind whirling.

"And what have you been doing all this time?" she murmured, petting his smooth black-and-red fur.

The boat thudded against the shore, bumping against the sand. Roseabelle turned to the group. "Jessicana's patch-ups won't last for long and the Darvonians are close behind us. We're going to have to abandon the boat and start looking for my father straightaway."

"I'll scout for anything suspicious," Jessicana volunteered, and Roseabelle agreed wholeheartedly. If they were going to explore an abandoned mystery island, a bird's eye view would be helpful.

Astro took the spyglass from her and peered into

it. "We really have to hurry! The Darvonians will be here in a matter of minutes."

"What?" Roseabelle exclaimed. That couldn't be true. Hadn't the Darvonians been way behind? She peered at the ocean, putting a hand over her forehead and blocking the sun from her eyes. Sure enough, the boats were moving swiftly toward the three friends, easily tracing the path Roseabelle and Astro had blasted.

"Hurry!" she said. "Astro, grab our supplies. Jessicana, scout the area. I'll take Moonstar and start searching in the trees." Roseabelle hurriedly surveyed the island, then pointed to a large brown cliff in the distance. "We'll meet there. Now go, go, go!"

"Good luck," Jessicana and Astro said at the same time, then all three of them scurried their separate ways.

JESSICANA IMMEDIATELY TRANSFORMED INTO A parrot and fluttered away, soaring high above the green treetops, swooping through the clear blue sky. She tried to stay within the white fluffy clouds so the Darvonians wouldn't see her.

Metamordia was enormous. But as Jessicana flew, she could see no signs of natives living there—and no Darvonians either. There was, however, an abundance of animals creeping, crawling, and flying about, so she knew that the island wasn't deserted. Looking down, she could see Roseabelle and Astro panting as they ran after her, crashing through masses of rich green bushes and trees.

Jessicana landed swiftly on the smooth brown cliff, ruffling her wings anxiously. Where could Magford be imprisoned? This island definitely did not look as though Darvonians had taken over it. She wondered if the Darvonians following them had landed on the island yet. The thought sent chills tingling down her spine. Parrots didn't seem to be common on this island. What if they recognized her for who she was?

Surveying the island, Jessicana compared Benotripia and Metamordia. It was strange how two things could be so different yet so amazing. Listening contentedly to the rush of the crystal waterfall, she marveled at how different it was from the one that had guarded the Stones of Horsh. This water was so clear and so pure, Jessicana could see straight through it.

She swooped down and looked through it, then squawked in surprise.

Was that a black stone behind the waterfall? Jessicana inched closer to the perilous rush of water, her sharp parrot eyes scrutinizing the waterfall. Beyond the falls, a strong sheen of black stood out. Her curiosity shot sky high.

Taking a deep breath, Jessicana flew straight through the water. Her wings became waterlogged and she gasped for breath. Transforming back into a girl in midair, her fingers latched on to a sharp protruding black rock.

And then Jessicana realized what was behind the waterfall.

She saw a wall of black stone with a small ledge precariously jutting out. Jessicana was relieved to see that no Darvonians or Metamordians were around to witness or report her being there. At least, she didn't see anyone.

Her blonde hair was soaked, and she figured she had better let herself dry off or when she transformed, her wings would be waterlogged. Jessicana found handholds and footholds and descended the wall of black stone carefully, looking around for anything unusual.

Her hand slipped and she caught herself, a small shriek escaping her lips. That was close. Even though she could transform into a parrot, flying with wet wings wouldn't be the greatest option. She'd probably have to walk back. Grasping onto the slippery rock, she cautiously descended a bit more, forcing herself not to look down.

Suddenly Jessicana found her foot swinging in midair as she searched for a foothold. Her stomach leaped into her throat. Did the wall of black stone end right here? Peeking down, she looked over the terrain.

Although the wall continued down, she could see an open crevasse right below her. She was glad she was used to heights; otherwise, she might have fallen the twenty feet to the ground. Carefully, she lowered herself using only her arms, her hands shaking uncontrollably, searching for a lower foothold. But she couldn't find anything, and her feet dangled in the open air.

Jessicana had to get around this certain crevasse or she knew she'd never make it to the ground. "I should've gone back to find Astro and Roseabelle," she said to herself, taking a calming breath. But already her sweaty fingers were slipping from the ledge. "No, no, come on. Keep yourself up," she whispered. As she grasped for a better handhold, her hands slipped, and she plummeted toward the ground, her stomach leaping into her throat.

And then she stopped. Jessicana realized with a *thump* that she'd landed on solid ground. She looked up and recognized the spot she'd been positioned at— only four feet above where she was now. Yet she was still surrounded by black stone. She'd landed on a flat ledge, overlooking the rocky pool that the waterfall gushed into.

Turning her head, an astounding sight awaited her gaze. It was an archway, tall and outlined by stones, fitting completely into the black cliffside. Jessicana observed the ledge she was standing on. It was particularly wide and rather thick. She jumped carefully on it a couple times. Obviously, it could hold a lot of weight.

Deciding she'd wait for Roseabelle and Astro, Jessicana sat down on the ledge, suspecting that if she went to try and find them, she might lose this particular spot on the waterfall. It was rather discreet. Finally, she saw a blurred shape through the waterfall. "ASTRO! ROSEABELLE!" Jessicana shouted. She repeatedly yelled their names until her voice became hoarse. A few moments of silence passed by.

There was a flash of silver and Astro stepped out from the torrent of water, coughing and sputtering. Jessicana doubted he'd ever be dry again. "Jessicana?" he asked. The two remaining backpacks—one had been lost in the rock spire graveyard—were slung over his shoulders.

"Up here!" she called. A few seconds later, she spotted a blurred shape nearing the waterfall once again. "ROSEABELLE!"

Jessicana rubbed her sore throat. Roseabelle eventually emerged with Moonstar by her side. The animal shook his fur out, sending droplets of water in every direction. Roseabelle squeezed out her mess of saturated locks and a stream of water erupted from them. "I never want to be wet again," she sputtered.

"Never mind that. I found some sort of tunnel!" Jessicana announced. "We can hide here and figure out a plan to find Magford."

"Great, but how are we going to get up there?" Astro asked. "We can't exactly fly like you." Beside him, Moonstar scaled the rock with bounding leaps, causing Jessicana to jump as he landed on the ledge. "And we aren't wild animals," he added, glaring at Moonstar.

Jessicana thought for a moment, tapping her chin. Suddenly, she straightened. "Roseabelle, use your Fur Beam," she suggested, thinking back to when her friend had transformed into a giant hairy beast. "That way you can boost Astro up, then turn back to your normal self and we can help you up."

"What?" Roseabelle groaned.

Astro looked away, and Jessicana suspected he was trying not to burst out laughing.

"Oh, be nice, Astro," Jessicana chided and he turned back, biting his lip.

"Sorry, Roseabelle," he said, but Jessicana could see his mouth still quivering as he stifled a laugh.

Roseabelle sighed and moved to the corner of the rock wall where tiny rays of sunshine were seeping through. She rolled up her sleeve and held up the sickly yellow spot on her elbow. A bright flash of light nearly blinded them, and Jessicana clapped a hand over her eyes.

"Please look away, Astro," Roseabelle's deep growly voice stated, and he obediently did what he was told. Jessicana's eyes opened just a crack. Sure enough, her friend was a couple of feet taller, covered in fur, and had gnarly claws. Astro tried to close his eyes and stumbled toward her but ended up smacking into the black wall of stone.

"A little help here?" he asked. Jessicana guided him verbally over to Roseabelle. "I think I'm permanently blind."

Jessicana giggled. "You'll be fine, Astro!"

With Astro riding piggyback, Roseabelle moved from her crouched state and into her full height. Astro blinked, opened his eyes, and climbed off her back onto the ledge next to Moonstar. Below them, Roseabelle shone her yellow spot in the sun again and reverted back into a girl.

Moonstar waited patiently for them as Jessicana

tapped her chin thoughtfully. "Hey, Astro, grab onto my ankles and lower me down. I'll help Roseabelle up."

"What?" he asked. "It's too far down. Can you even reach her?"

Jessicana scrutinized their surroundings and realized that Roseabelle was at least fifteen feet away from them. Astro was right; it wasn't going to work. She glanced down at her ring, pushing the Grapplegore's emerald button. Instantly two ropes sprang, one dropping toward Roseabelle. "Hold on!" she shouted.

Roseabelle tied the rope around her waist, then began to scale the rock. Jessicana assisted her climb by pulling on the rope as much as she could. Roseabelle ascended rather smoothly, although she tripped a couple of times. Thanks to the Grapplegore, though, she stayed clinging to the rocky cliff side.

Roseabelle made it up the cliff and untied the rope from her waist. "Thanks, Jessicana," she said, out of breath.

"Are the Darvonians close behind?" Jessicana asked.

"They're on the island near here," Astro reported. "We need to be careful; I had a close call. When I was leaving, they were just docking on the edge of the island."

Abruptly and without a single noise, the animal slunk into the shadows, disappearing into the tunnel hole. Jessicana's eyes widened in alarm.

"Moonstar, come back here!" Astro hissed but the creature just kept on going.

"So, we follow?" Jessicana asked, glancing skeptically at the darkness that awaited them.

"We follow," Roseabelle agreed and stepped ahead, weapon at her side.

CHAPTER 9

Darvonian Caverns

STEPPING INTO THE PITCH-BLACK CAVERN, Roseabelle and her friends followed the pattering of Moonstar's light steps. Pebbles crunched underfoot as they walked, and she winced with each noise. As if reading Roseabelle's thoughts, Jessicana said from behind, "Try not to make as much noise."

Moonstar abruptly halted in his tracks, and Astro nearly tumbled over him. There was a faint echo and Roseabelle stopped, nervously glancing into darkness, but she couldn't see anything. Taking a cautious step forward, she found her foot hanging in thin air. Was this some sort of precipice? She stared accusingly at

Moonstar. "This leads off a cliff edge," she said. "What are you trying to do, Moonstar?"

In response, he pushed her forward a bit, and Roseabelle yelped, then realized her foot had touched a solid surface. "It's a staircase," she muttered to herself in relief. Moonstar moved past Roseabelle and continued down the stairs. The three friends descended after him. But as the distant sound of rushing water faded, new noises flooded over them. It was the clash of wooden wagons and the simmering of lit torches.

As they reached the bottom of the staircase, a vibrant amber glow washed over them, and they all stopped short.

They had just entered a clearing, illuminated by dim torchlight. But it was enough to see that they were no longer alone. Hooded figures pushed stone vehicles forward on wheels, and the murmur of chatter and conversation echoed in the tunnels. Roseabelle could see smoking pits from where various lights danced, and the three friends, all at once, exchanged wide-eyed glances.

Darvonians.

But that wasn't the freakiest part. Relaxed and lying near the entrance was a monstrous creature with soft green skin and an enormous shell. Webbed nets lined with spikes covered its shell, which connected to a large head, wrinkly and gray. Its legs were short but thin and packed with muscle.

Luckily, the creature's eyes were closed.

Roseabelle, Jessicana, and Astro exchanged alarmed glances. Roseabelle hesitated. It wouldn't be wise to sneak past this creature. Where were they going? But they couldn't just abandon Moonstar. And besides, if he were seen by the Darvonians, they would be suspicious. Feeling a bit reluctant, she crept past the creature with Astro and Jessicana close behind. Roseabelle tried to keep calm, hoping that the animal wouldn't wake up. If he did, they would be done for.

The truth hit Roseabelle hard. The Darvonians had clearly been here for years, using this place as their secret hideout. But for what? And where were all the Metamordians?

Before any of the friends could talk to each other, Moonstar purred quietly, so soft that only they could hear. Then he darted behind a stack of tall barrels a few feet to their left, leaping into open sight for just a second. "Moonstar!" Jessicana whispered loudly, but the animal stayed where he was, shooting a pleading glance at Roseabelle.

"We need to follow him," Roseabelle whispered. They couldn't just stay here, crouched in a big huddle, waiting for the Darvonians to find them. "He knows what he's doing."

Rolling and ducking, Astro dashed behind the barrels, and Jessicana followed. Roseabelle crept after them, glad they had the cover of darkness on their side.

They continued traveling discreetly in this manner, Moonstar leading the way, and the three friends clambering after him. Luckily they'd had some experience keeping quiet before, and didn't make any suspicious noises. Leaping from one obstacle to the next, they managed to stay hidden in the shadows.

And then Astro's foot clanged against a metal shield resting on the ground. Roseabelle froze, heart pounding, as the clamor of hushed conversation suddenly halted behind them. But after a few painstaking seconds of suspense, the Darvonians resumed their work.

Not much security, she thought. She dug in her pack silently, withdrawing a sheathed sword that she had borrowed from Astro, as Moonstar directed them to a stop at a black stone wall. Up ahead, Jessicana pulled out a Spidegar, and Astro armed himself with a Trapita, a rod with three blades lined on it. Any moment they could be discovered, and they had to be ready for an attack.

Roseabelle saw the creature take another step forward. Up ahead, Jessicana took in a sharp breath.

Roseabelle blinked a couple of times when she realized that Moonstar had disappeared. One minute he'd been there, right in front of them, and the next he had melted into the shadows.

"Where'd he go?" Astro muttered frantically and crawled forward. Then, Astro was gone too.

"It's a portal!" Jessicana realized, keeping her voice low. "Come on." She moved forward and then vanished from sight. Roseabelle winced, glancing back. Well, what did she have to lose? She could only hope that on the other side, her father really was waiting.

Inhaling deeply to calm her nerves, Roseabelle stepped forward as a light-headed, dizzying sensation enveloped her.

When she opened her eyes, she only met darkness. "Roseabelle?" said a voice to her right. *Jessicana.*

"Where are we?" she asked. A silver-blue glow flared inside the room from Astro's crackling fingertips. Roseabelle could now see that they were in some sort of black hall. The worn stones they stood on were covered in slash-and-burn marks, as though weapons had been forged here.

"Moonstar went this way," Astro's voice said. With the small amount of light, she could see his faint outline. "Everyone okay?"

"Yes," Jessicana said, and Roseabelle echoed her.

"This way," Astro said, and the girls made an effort to follow his footsteps, because he was the only one with light. Roseabelle scanned their environment, taking in every little detail in case they needed to make a quick getaway.

"He's stopped," Astro reported.

Roseabelle put a hand on her sword. An eerie feeling sent chills tingling down her. Could it be possible that someone was watching them? "And now he's turning a corner and—" His voice broke off in the empty blackness. Jessicana crossed over to him, treading lightly.

"What—" Jessicana tried to say, but Astro clapped a hand over her mouth. Roseabelle swallowed and quickly caught up with her friends. Obviously, something unpleasant was right there.

Astro slowly took his hand from Jessicana's mouth. By the light of his crackling fingertips, Roseabelle could see a long corridor with at least six metal doors guarded by a mass of about twenty Darvonians. Fortunately, Jessicana and Astro had been whispering, and the Darvonians hadn't been really paying attention. It was clear that they didn't expect intruders to find their secret hideout, maybe because no one had ever showed up that they'd needed to fight. Roseabelle again wondered just how long the Darvonians had been secretly encamped down here.

"We need to get into the open and knock them out," Astro mouthed. Roseabelle shook her head. They were three kids against twenty grown Darvonians. Even with their powers, it was a challenge. And if even one of the Darvonians escaped, they would be in serious trouble.

"No," she mouthed back. "I have a better idea."

Bending down in the dirt, she drew a diagram with her finger, outlining the plan. Slowly, her friends' faces lit up.

A few minutes later, they were all ready, each standing in a different position in the corridor. Jessicana had a Spidegar from Astro's pack and was crouched at the far end of the hall, around a corner. Roseabelle herself waited at the opposite end of the hall in the same position, her sword ready.

Astro, lying flat on his stomach, looked to Roseabelle, who nodded. Suddenly a stream of silver blue lightning flew from Astro's fingertips—right at the Darvonian guards.

Lightning crackled in every direction. It was just as Roseabelle had predicted—pandemonium. Already she could see six Darvonians lying unconscious. Their armor had protected them from further injury. Another Darvonian who had escaped the brunt of Astro's attack raced out of the corridor blindly, frantically attempting to get out. Jessicana quickly wrapped him in the webs of her Spidegar, entangling him fully. Astro shot a separate bolt of lightning at him as well, and soon the hooded figure was out cold.

In a matter of minutes, all twenty Darvonians were facedown and unconscious. Standing, Roseabelle quickly searched them, but found no keys. "Do you think my father is behind one of these doors?" she asked, and Jessicana shrugged.

"Most likely. Moonstar seems to know what he's doing." Inspecting the doors closely, Roseabelle took a few steps back. They were made of a certain kind of metal and had no barred windows to look inside. But to her left, Moonstar whined and crouched at a door at the end of the corridor. It was tinier than the others, with no keyhole.

"How do we get in?" Astro asked.

Roseabelle sighed, wondering what she could do and which powers she could use. Dust Draining? It would have no effect. Fur Beam? It could be useful, but there was no sunlight here to allow her to morph. Telekinesis? There was no way she could remove a door that heavy.

Suddenly, the trio heard the faint echo of voices from behind them, and they exchanged worried glances. The Darvonians must have heard the commotion. They had to get inside before they were found!

Moonstar clawed at the hinges. Astro dug in his pack, then began hacking at them with a Dragocone Ray. The metal began to dent slightly, but even the force of a powerful weapon couldn't break the hinges. "Wait," Astro said as he dug in his pack again and brought out a heavy Flame-hurler.

"But that could cause an explosion," Roseabelle protested as he loaded extra force ammo onto the Flame-hurler and leveled it at the door.

"What if Magford's behind the door?" Jessicana pointed out. "And if the Darvonians come through, we can't lock the door on them."

Astro sighed. "You're right." He slid the Flame-hurler back inside.

Roseabelle studied the hinges frantically as the sound of clonking heavy footsteps became even louder. She noticed something on the silver hinges. "They have slits!" she exclaimed. "Astro, shoot your lightning between the openings in the hinges."

"What?" Jessicana exclaimed.

"It'll work," Roseabelle assured them. "It'll break the hinges open, and once we're in, we can bar the door from the inside. We have to be quick, though. I can use my telekinesis to help too."

"Well, it's better than exploding everything," Jessicana agreed. They took a step back to allow Astro to step forward. Quick as a flash, three bolts of precise lightning shot through the hinges and the door fell forward. Just before it hit the ground, Roseabelle clenched her teeth and froze the door in midair with her telekinesis, strength draining from her limbs.

Astro and Jessicana raced forward to grab the door, and they caught it inches before it hit the ground. "Go!" Astro urged. Roseabelle leaped past them into the dank musty interior of, hopefully, where Magford was being held.

Moonstar followed her, trotting alongside obediently. "You okay?" Roseabelle asked as Jessicana and Astro lifted the door back into its proper place.

"Yeah," Jessicana said, brushing her blonde locks out of her face. "We'll stay here, just in case the Darvonians try to enter." She touched Roseabelle's arm. "Good luck."

Roseabelle smiled. "Thanks." Swallowing her fear, she turned the corner, ready to face whatever would come next.

CHAPTER 10

Tropsyle

ROSEABELLE REALIZED THIS CELL WAS A LOT larger than a normal one would be. It wasn't just a single room; winding corridors, fake doors, and windows twisted all around her. Moonstar rubbed against her leg. "How do I find him in this place?" she whispered, and the animal bounded forward. "Wait up!" she called and ran after Moonstar, following him through rapidly twisting passages.

Moonstar stepped into an even darker room than before, and Roseabelle cautiously followed, an unexpected flash of friendly warmth filling her being.

The room was full of scrolls and ink, the pleasant aroma of a library drifting in the air. A few rugs lay on the floor and a small bed was pushed in the corner of the room. In the center of it all was a man dressed in a ratty brown shirt with raggedy pants and worn sandals. His back was facing her, and he was writing furiously on a piece of trutan with an ink-tipped quill. What Roseabelle noticed most of all was the large mop of curly red hair spread all over his head. A dirty black chain was connected from his ankle to the wall.

Hearing her hesitant footsteps, he turned around. He had a red beard as well, Roseabelle noted. His eyebrows scrunched together. and he bore a striking resemblance to Dastrock. "Huh. Didn't know they sent IBs down here anymore." His voice was warm but firm and gentle at the same time. Roseabelle grimaced at the mention of IBs—the term stood for Imitation Benotripian, Darvonians who resembled Benotripians.

Roseabelle took a few steps closer and incredible warmth filled her chest. Could it be? She had to pinch herself to make sure that this really wasn't a dream. "It's really you," she said, a relieved smile spreading over her features. Magford had gone missing when she was very young, and Danette had been left to rule Benotripia all alone. All Roseabelle's life she'd dreamed about what her father would look like, and here he was, right in front of her.

"Sorry, I don't think we've met before. As I told Sheklyth, these scrolls aren't really worth scouring. No information for you here." Magford talked to her, turning back around and Roseabelle understood. Of course. The last time he'd seen her was when she was two years old.

"I'm not an IB," she said, taking a tentative step closer to him.

"Metamordian then? Fellow prisoner?"

"Not exactly. My name's Roseabelle." She didn't know what else to say, desperately hoping he'd remember her name.

Magford slowly pivoted to face her, his expression mesmerized. "Now that's a name I haven't heard in a very long time." Roseabelle swallowed as he took a quick breath. "I can see Danette in you . . . that face . . . and that hair . . . It's not possible . . . Roseabelle?" He said each word slowly as if he was staring at a ghost.

Roseabelle choked back tears of happiness and leaped forward, embracing her father as he looked into her face, shaking his head in disbelief. "I-I've been thinking, dreaming about you ever since they took me away from Benotripia," Magford said, holding Roseabelle close. "I can't believe it! You're really here! I—" His voice broke off, trembling with emotion as they hugged each other. Roseabelle closed her eyes, solidifying this moment in her mind and vowing to never let it go. They held on for a long time—it seemed like years to Roseabelle.

They broke apart and Roseabelle stared at all of the objects around them. "I don't get it. Why do you have all these scrolls and furniture?"

Magford chuckled and gestured to the chain on his ankle, which Roseabelle realized was actually extremely lengthy. Part of the black links coiled in an enormous pile. "They let me roam around free in this entire maze. It used to be a lot of junk, kind of like a storage area. I turned it into this." He gestured to the room. "And of course, my power of supersonic speed did help."

Roseabelle stared around in wonder. "Wow, you really did make some amazing things. Why didn't they confiscate all this?"

"They were hoping I'd write some secret plans on the parchment, maybe give some clues to what the Benotripians were planning, communicate with the outside world. I knew too much, you see. That's why they brought me here. And ever since, they've basically forgotten about me, except for a few occasions." Magford shook his head. "Roseabelle, you've put yourself in grave danger by coming here. How did you get here?"

Just then, Moonstar appeared, melting out of the shadows, and Roseabelle jumped in surprise. She'd completely forgotten the creature was even there.

"Of course." Magford laughed and Moonstar tread up to him. The man stroked his ears. "The last thing I told this little guy was to find you. I can telepathically communicate with animals, you know."

"You can?" Roseabelle asked, astonished. Danette had really never talked about Magford's abilities.

Magford nodded. "He probably was a stowaway on a Darvonian ship or something. We share a special bond—Moonstar has been my personal companion for a very long time. He's a Sheilvoh, part of a rare species with extraordinary powers." He shook his head. "But why didn't Danette stop you from coming? How did you even leave Benotripia?"

"It's a long story and we'll get to that later, but we need to get you out of here," Roseabelle said. To her horror, the clashing of metal and sound of angry yelling echoed in the caverns. "The Darvonians found us," she whispered. "Of course they'd know to look here." She circled around the chain. "What are your other powers?" she asked, examining it closely.

"Shadow tumbling, camouflaging myself into my surroundings, Bubble building, lots of others too. But none can get me out of this chain. Believe me I've tried. And besides there's no way I could get past the Tropjyle."

"Tropjyle?" Roseabelle asked, inquisitive.

"The monstrous reptile guarding the front," Magford pointed out. "It can hurl its nets at lightning speed and the barbs attached to those things are deathly poisonous. You get caught in one of those, and it's all over."

"So obviously, don't wake the giant monster," Roseabelle said, taking a shaky breath. Her eyes drifted back to the chain. She knew a sledge hammer or a large axe should cut it, but she didn't have the time to draw one on the trutan. Wait a second. "What's this chain made of?" she asked.

Magford grasped her shoulders. "Roseabelle, you need to leave now. Shadow tumble out of here! I don't matter. You can come back later."

"No, I can't," she said. "I can't leave my friends behind."

"What? You're not alone?" Right on cue, Jessicana and Astro came bursting in, breathing heavily.

"The Darvonians found us," Jessicana wheezed. "We blocked the door with a few crates we found in a different room, but it won't last long."

"We need to get out of here!" Astro exclaimed.

"Astro!" Roseabelle said. She turned to her father.

"Do you think lightning would slice through the chain?"

Magford raised his eyebrows. "Uh, lightning?"

"Quick, Astro," Roseabelle said, glancing at the other passageways. "It's worth a try." Astro bent down and carefully examined the chain from Magford's ankle.

"Look away!" Astro announced and everyone shielded their faces. There was a flash of silver and blue, and the chain thudded to the ground. Magford quickly gathered up his scrolls in a bundle, tucking them under his arm.

"Thank you," he said to Astro. "Are you armed with weapons?"

Astro nodded and quickly handed Magford double swords. "How do we get out now?" Jessicana asked frantically. Roseabelle quickly slung her backpack from her shoulder and set it on the ground, rummaging inside. Just then they heard the door knocked over by the furious Darvonians.

"I have an idea," she said. "Obviously our cover's blown, so we can't use the element of surprise. That means," she continued, withdrawing a Flame-hurler from her backpack and loading it with ammo balls, "we need to cause an explosion." She grinned at the shocked Astro and Jessicana. "Everyone back!"

She pulled the trigger and three missiles shot

straight at the metal wall, exploding in a mass of fire and smoke, shaking the entire room. Coughing, Roseabelle squinted through the smoke. Sure enough, a gaping hole had been blown into the wall, revealing the Darvonian hideout they had been in earlier.

"Run!" Astro yelled as the Darvonians in the hideout brandished glowing weapons. As Jessicana followed him, Magford glanced at Roseabelle, shaking his head.

"When did you grow up so fast?"

Then they plunged into battle. Roseabelle reached into her pack, retrieved a spear for herself, and zipped it closed. Astro was rapidly shooting lightning bolts at a group of Darvonians and Jessicana was jabbing a Thepgile at two hooded figures, holding them back for now.

As a Darvonian thrust a Trapita at Roseabelle, she blocked the blow with her spear, throwing him back against the wall. She ducked as another one swung a Dragocone Ray at her, rolling and thwacking him in the legs with the spear, sending him sprawling.

Out of the corner of her eye, she caught a glimpse of her father. For someone who'd been cooped up in a prison for years, he fought extremely well. Jabbing, slicing, blocking, and thrusting, Magford battled against at least thirty Darvonians, using his supersonic speed.

They tried to fight back, but whenever they swung at them, he was already in a different spot.

Suddenly a monstrous roar echoed through the caverns and everyone froze—Darvonians, Benotripians, and Magford and Roseabelle, who were Metamordians. By the light of the dim torches, Roseabelle could see a wrinkly head rise above the throngs of people, and she backed up slowly.

The Tropjyle had awakened.

The Darvonians instantly dispersed, but they were too late—the creature shifted its shell and five nets sprang out, catching a few cloaked figures in their grasp. It was obvious that the monster was feeling threatened and was now protecting itself.

Roseabelle noticed its feet were built for sprinting fast and she backed up. The Darvonians screamed as the creature released nets in every direction, trapping many figures. She had an urge to grab her friends and father and dart up the stairs, but the monster was blocking their path.

The annoyed Tropjyle's eyes suddenly locked onto Astro, and it advanced toward him. The monstrous footsteps shook the entire tunnel, rattling the ground and causing a cloud of dust to float down from the ceiling. The Tropjyle's piercing stare swept over them, and Roseabelle suddenly froze, paralyzed by fear.

Several other Darvonians were suffering the same effect. It was obviously a quality this reptile possessed.

Roseabelle watched in horror as the monster thundered over to Astro, rearing back and preparing to lash the lightning boy into its trap.

"Hey!" Jessicana abruptly yelled, waving her arms in front of the Tropjyle, and Roseabelle jumped, breaking out of the trance. The huge creature swiveled its head, eyes narrowing in on Jessicana. Roseabelle barely had time to wonder how her friend had gotten out of the Tropjyle's paralyzing effect, before the enormous foot of the monster rose over her. In its path toward Jessicana, the Tropjyle was ready to lumber right over Roseabelle. She leaped out of the way just in time as it came crashing down, sending her flying against the back wall.

The next thing Roseabelle knew, a sharp pain had pierced her skull and her head lolled back, her vision blurry and distant. A hand touched her arm and she struggled to focus her vision. "Roseabelle!" said a voice beside her and she blinked. Her father was crouching beside her, looking concerned. It took Roseabelle a minute to get her bearings before she could look at the battle playing before her. Astro and Jessicana were fighting the Tropjyle—lightning peppered the monster and a brightly colored bird circled it, pecking its leathery head. The creature shot numerous nets at Astro, but he dodged—unfortunately his sword wasn't so lucky. Roseabelle saw one net curl around the sword and wrench it from Astro's hand. The weapon clattered to the floor, wrapped up within poisonous barbs.

Jessicana dove away from the Tropjyle and zoomed toward Roseabelle, transforming back into a girl. "Roseabelle!" she exclaimed. She dug in her pack and brought out her mini potion kit. As a healer, Jessicana carried potions with her wherever she went.

The Darvonians had switched tactics and were coming toward them now, but Roseabelle was too dazed to say anything. Magford noticed something was awry and pivoted, slashing his double swords at the cloaked figures. He was like a whirlwind of fury.

Jessicana hurriedly mixed a frothy blue liquid and a white powder together, then shoved the contents into Roseabelle's mouth. Her senses immediately sharpened, and Roseabelle jolted up, warmth and energy trickling into her limbs. Moonstar suddenly leaped out from the shadows, sinking its knife-like teeth into the monster's leg and the Tropjyle howled. Roseabelle saw the Tropjyle's head retracting into its shell. It really was threatened now and was resorting to the only other way to protect itself. Another group of Darvonians was advancing on Astro, backing him into a corner.

"Thanks, Jessicana," she said and her friend nodded.

"There's no time to waste, come on, we have to get out of here!" Jessicana said.

A different throng of Darvonians rushed at the girls, and Roseabelle blocked one from striking with her Trapita and dodged another blow from a sword. Jessicana swung her javelin and knocked a Darvonian aside. The two then joined hands, running toward Astro.

But by the time they got there, his fingertips were crackling. The Darvonians who had ambushed him lay on the floor, out cold. Astro grinned and Jessicana muttered, "Show off."

The three of them turned toward Magford, and Roseabelle's blood ran ice cold. The Darvonians were closing in around him. To her relief, he sped around them—only to come face-to-face with another group.

"Dad!" she called. The word felt foreign but special on her tongue. She hadn't said that, well, in as long as she could remember, ever. "We need to get out of here!" Magford's gaze turned to the staircase and Moonstar raced between the Darvonians, bounding up the stone stairs.

"I'll meet you at the top," she promised her friends.

Roseabelle dashed to a shadowy corner, closed her eyes, and pictured the shadow of the cave entrance.

In a whirling sensation, she was there, right at the top of the staircase. Magford, her friends, and Moonstar were rushing up the stairs below her. "Hurry!" she yelled. Her friends looked surprised at how quickly she had shadow tumbled, but they followed her advice, running up the staircase and skidding to a stop on the ledge of the cave entrance.

"Hurry, get on Moonstar!" Magford urged. "He can carry three kids your weight quite a long distance."

"How? And won't we just crash below? Wait—can he *fly*?"

"Not exactly," Magford said and touched Roseabelle's cheek. "Get away from here. I'll be with you in a few minutes. Trust me."

"Wait, back to Benotripia?" she asked, confused.

"No, Darvonia," he said. With that, he turned away. Jessicana and Roseabelle clambered onto the enormous creature. Roseabelle didn't exactly doubt that Moonstar couldn't carry them—he was huge—but he couldn't fly! Both of the girls heard the raging cries of the Darvonians close behind them, and Magford motioned for Astro to get on.

Just then, a Darvonian emerged from below, drawing a knife, and Roseabelle yelled, "Astro! Behind you!"

CHAPTER 11
A Plan

ONE SECOND ASTRO WAS READY TO CLIMB onto Moonstar; the next he heard the clink of metal whizzing through the air.

Instinctively, he ducked and rolled. A dagger flew past just where his head had been, disappearing into the waterfall. A Darvonian stood by the staircase, completely hooded and holding a Dragocone Ray. Astro quickly dived for the Darvonian's ankle, tripping him, just as he was about to bring down the Ray on top of him.

The Darvonian landed in a heap on the ledge and Astro hurriedly jumped onto the animal. Worried, he turned to look back at Magford, who swung his double swords as he eyed the new attacker. Roseabelle's father then sank into the black camouflage behind him. Astro blinked a couple of times. If he hadn't been staring at Magford moments before, he wouldn't have known where he was.

"Moonstar will know where to take you! I'll catch up," Magford promised. As the Darvonians suddenly poured from the cave entrance, he began battling their Dragocone Rays, breaking their Trapitas in half, dismantling their Spidegars before they got a chance to even throw at him.

"Now, Moonstar!" Jessicana urged, and the Sheilvoh leaped off the ledge.

The wind whistled in Astro's ears, barrelling past him, an eerie whooshing sound filling the air.

The three friends screamed, closing their eyes as the ground came closer, but the impact never came. Astro opened his eyes—they were on the stone floor. This didn't make sense. He leaned over to look at the ground and realized Moonstar's paws weren't even touching the stone.

He's so fast he doesn't even touch the ground, Astro realized in awe. The three friends hung on as Moonstar carried them through the waterfall. The clear liquid came rushing down on them, and Astro coughed and tried to splash it out of his face.

Sputtering out water, Jessicana groaned. "Really?" Astro reckoned that was the third time she'd been soaked that day.

As they headed toward the ocean, Astro braced himself. Was Moonstar hiding some other secret power? Maybe he could lift a little higher in the air and fly? But as they left the ground, the friends felt ocean spray hitting their faces. It suddenly came to Astro—*Moonstar is so fast he can run on water.*

This was more exhilarating than anything he'd ever experienced, and he let out a whoop. Roseabelle reached out her hand to catch the salty sea spray, laughing as they sped across the ocean. It was unbelievable to be traveling so fast—Astro had never felt so free in his life.

But he suddenly realized he wouldn't feel free for long.

They were on their way to Darvonia.

SHADOWY FOG HUNG OVER BLACKWATER SEA as Moonstar sprinted across the water, the dark island coming within the three friends' view. "What if they see us?" Astro asked.

"I don't know," Jessicana said, tucking a strand of blonde hair behind her ear with a trembling hand. "But Danette and Dastrock should be safe, maybe hiding away. At the worst, they've been captured. The Darvonians would want them alive."

Astro could tell Roseabelle was trying to keep her doubt and fear hidden away. He put a hand on her shoulder. "It's going to be all right."

Roseabelle gave him a small smile but turned away, her muscles still tense. Moonstar suddenly put on a burst of speed as they neared the coast of Darvonia. Astro reeled backward, his vision blurring as Moonstar shot forward.

Moonstar skidded to a halt, and all three friends sprawled on the rocky beach, groaning. The Sheilvoh nudged them as if urging them to move on. Reluctantly, they all stood up and followed him to a small rock cranny, where an underground passage opened up.

The three friends sat down and broke out their remaining food, spilling two loaves and a collection of fruit on the ground. Astro gathered up all the food he could eat, completely famished. They had been so focused on rescuing Magford that they hadn't eaten in two days.

Suddenly from the shadows, Roseabelle's father appeared, and they all jumped back. Magford was covered in cuts and bruises, and his daughter gasped. "Are you all right?" she asked, leaping to her feet.

"I'm fine, Roseabelle," Magford said, embracing her quickly. "But, first, I must tell you what is going on. The secret I'm about to reveal is the reason the Darvonians captured me—I knew too much. So once I pass this information down to you, you must be careful. Understood?"

Astro's heartbeat picked up a bit, and he stared at Roseabelle's father with intrigue.

"What exactly do you know about the Dream World?" Magford asked.

Astro shifted in his seat, and his friends did the same as they exchanged glances. They recalled when Asteran, Jessicana's former trainer, had dropped a feather on the ground that Roseabelle had then picked up. She had entered into the Dream World. "Well, I accidentally traveled there a while ago," Roseabelle said, and Magford's eyebrows shot up.

Jessicana handed him Horsh's papers. "We found these in the ground near Astro's home," she said. "They looked pretty authentic to us and they had Horsh's mark on them, so we were certain the author was telling the truth."

Magford cleared his throat, looking over them. "Yes. These are mine actually."

"What?" Astro asked. Roseabelle's father was making no sense.

"Well, yes, they are Horsh's, but I excavated them from the ground. It's how I learned about the Dream World." Magford gestured to the point where the words stopped. "I smudged that over so the Darvonians wouldn't learn where the entrance to the Dream World was."

"So when the Darvonians captured you . . . ?" Astro began.

"Yes, when I found this they became incredibly suspicious. When they found out I had learned where the Dream World's entrance was, they came after me. Luckily I had already rubbed those words away and buried the trutan in a place I thought was safe." He raised his eyebrows. "How did you find this anyway?"

"Well, I fell from the sky and my lightning went off," Astro said, his tone nonchalant. "And then we kind of found it."

Roseabelle's father gaped at him. "Clearly, I've missed a lot over the past few years. Do you mind informing me a bit?" And so they did, telling Magford of all the adventures they had experienced, how they had rescued Danette from the Darvonians and how they had obtained the Stones of Horsh. Astro noticed Magford's eyes slightly moistened when they talked about Danette.

Jessicana withdrew the spyglass. "Is this yours too?"

Magford's eyes lit up. "Resourceful children! This is the Third Eye. It belongs to the rightful ruler of Benotripia—and it really is an useful artifact. I was scouting the Dream World, when they came. Moonstar was with me and I silently communicated with him that he should run back to Metamordia. I don't know what he was thinking when he found you, Roseabelle. Maybe he had sensed your presence near when he was out on the ocean, and traced you to Benotripia."

"So, where is the entrance to the Dream World?" Astro asked, but Magford held up a hand.

"I'd rather not say it out loud. Do you have the Stones?"

Astro reached into his pocket and patted the bloodred Stone. Jessicana nodded as well. Roseabelle slid her hand inside her tunic pocket, then froze. Frantically, she dug her hands into both her pockets, scrambling around, mouth agape.

"What is it?" Magford asked.

She held up her pocket and Astro saw a large hole in the bottom. "My Stone," Roseabelle exclaimed. "It's gone!"

Magford swallowed. "Well, that does present a problem." He slid his swords back into their sheaths. Drumming the hilts on the ground, he sat in concentrated thought for a few minutes. The three friends exchanged glances. They couldn't destroy the Dream World without Roseabelle's Stone!

"Wait," he said, flipping his swords into the air and catching them by the hilt. "I've got it! There's a high point in Darvonia where we could attract Roseabelle's Stone. Horsh originally wanted to hide them separately but it didn't work. All three are connected to each other. So if we touch those two together at a high peak, the third will magnetically float to it."

Astro grinned. "Awesome! Let's go!"

Magford shook his head. "It's not that easy. Darvonians will be patrolling everywhere. And it will be tiring for you two."

"We can fight through them," Jessicana said.

"We're a team," Roseabelle added.

Magford bit the inside of his cheek. "Listen, I can't just leave you here. You're children!"

"Yeah, but we've been through a lot," Astro said. "We rescued the ruler of Benotripia by ourselves. Now we just need to fight off a mass army of Darvonians. Plus we have a magical animal and a warrior dude by our side. We'll do just fine."

Roseabelle nodded. "Trust us."

"But is the entrance to the Dream World far from here?" Jessicana inquired.

Magford sighed. "It would be a three days' walk from here, maybe farther. But with Moonstar? A few minutes tops. We just need to evade a lot of Darvonians."

Roseabelle and Jessicana jumped to their feet, sorting through the backpacks and picking out weapons. Astro walked up to Magford. "Um, sir?" He pulled out his Stone. "Our Stones aren't working. It's like they lost their power ever since we left Benotripia."

To his surprise, Magford chuckled. "Horsh bewitched them to only exercise their power while in Benotripia or when near the Dream World. He didn't want the Darvonians to be able to use them freely on the island."

Roseabelle and Jessicana had overheard. "So, what will destroying the Dream World do to the Darvonians?" the daughter asked her father.

Magford put a hand on her shoulder. "Destroying the Dream World with the Stones of Horsh will demolish the Stones as well. Also, the Darvonians' power will decrease, their fear won't be as strong. They'll withdraw from Metamordia as the Benotripians advance on them. We'll free the people there." He gestured wildly with his hands as he spoke, and Astro could tell he was beyond elated.

Magford turned to the kids. "But the Dream World will be dangerous."

Astro frowned. "Why? Isn't it just empty?"

The Metamordian shook his head. "No, not exactly. Everything that that Stone has made disappear"—he gestured to Astro's jewel—"is in the Dream World."

Astro shook his head wildly and turned back to Roseabelle. Oh no, this was not good!

As Magford stepped ahead, Jessicana and Astro sidled up to Roseabelle. "You know what this means?" he asked her.

Roseabelle swallowed. "A lot of Darvonians will be in there?" she guessed.

"Well, that too, but Sheklyth is still alive!" Astro said. Roseabelle stared at her feet.

"We'll handle her," she said, forcing on a confident smile, but he could still tell she was beyond nervous.

"So we leave now?" Jessicana asked.

Magford seemed to consider it, then shook his head, pointing to the sky above. It was getting darker by the minute. "Darvonians relish the cover of darkness—it would not be wise. Let's stay here for the night." Magford nodded. "We leave tomorrow."

CHAPTER 12

Roarcaneum

MAGFORD SAT AT THE FRONT OF THE CAVE, half awake watching for intruders, and half asleep to get a bit of rest. Meanwhile, the three friends curled up in the back with Moonstar. Roseabelle had created sleeping rolls from the trutan, and Jessicana was curled up in one of them.

She couldn't believe everything that had happened—it was crazy. Brushing aside her mass of tangled blonde hair, Jessicana closed her eyes and made an effort to sleep. It felt nice to not be resting on a rocking boat that was being tossed among the waves.

Her fingers clutched tightly at her aqua blue Stone. Jessicana knew how important this was to the

Benotripians. They might have their strong defenses but with the Dream World, the Darvonians could appear on Benotripia *behind* the defenses, catching the Benotripians completely by surprise.

Dawn broke the horizon, and they all breathed a sigh of relief that no Darvonians had spotted them during the night. They all sat down to eat milk and nuts, stomachs rumbling with hunger.

"All right," Magford said, tapping a finger on his mostly bare chin. He had made an attempt to shave the beard off with a Trapita last night, which had left his beard a huge mess—all that remained was some ragged stubble. "Remember, we need to stay hidden. That's the key element here. This is life or death now. Stealth is the only option we have."

All of the friends gulped at the same time. "What's ahead of us?" Jessicana asked. "I mean, just the Darvonians themselves right?"

Magford grimaced. "I wish, but you know the Darvonians. Always full of surprises, whether you like it or not." He tossed each of them weapons: a Spidegar and javelin for Jessicana, a razor sharp Thepgile for Roseabelle, and a broadsword for Astro. "Weapons are great for defending yourselves, but you need to remember who you are—the Darvonians are all about weapons, fighting. But you are Benotripians,

Metamordians. You have powers and you have them for a reason. So if you have to choose between weapons and powers, choose who you really are." He paused. "Now, let's find Roseabelle's Stone. Come on."

THE FRIENDS CREPT TO THE EDGE OF THE CAVE AND Magford motioned to the outside. The air was filled with thick black smog, and the landscape was as rocky as Jessicana remembered. "If we're lucky enough, the Darvonians won't know we're here." He took a step out into the open and his foot instantly squelched in a patch of dark mud. Magford winced. "I would just Shadow Tumble but none of you would know where to go."

"There has to be a specific spot?" Jessicana asked, and he nodded.

"Yes," Magford said. "Also, a single person is easier to overcome than four." He continued walking through the spongy ground, which was much like a marsh.

"That's strange. The ground was dry last night," Roseabelle remarked and took a step forward, following her father. Astro did the same. That was when Jessicana noticed black sludge reaching up toward Magford's ankles.

"Everyone," Jessicana said uneasily. "What are you standing in?"

Magford glanced down and his face suddenly went very pale. "Oh no."

"What?" Astro asked.

"We need to get out of here!" Magford roared.

The ground began to tremor a bit and Magford tried to squirm out of the sludge. Jessicana watched, helpless, as her friends struggled.

Jessicana frantically scurried around the cave, searching for something she could pull her friends up with. Her eyes landed on a piece of thick, dark wood lying in the back of the cave, and she scrambled toward it. Jessicana's eyes were wide. She had a slight suspicion of what was going on, but was too scared to think about it.

"Is this quicksand?" Astro yelled.

"Worse!" Magford said as Jessicana held out the piece of wood. Roseabelle managed to grab onto it, and Jessicana clenched her teeth, pulling back on the thick wood.

"Come on," Roseabelle grunted, and Jessicana pulled as hard as she could—but it wasn't working. She jumped when the wood broke in half, leaving a woozy Roseabelle still sinking into the sludge. All three of Jessicana's comrades were now knee deep in the mud.

"Try stabbing it!" Magford said.

Astro cocked his head to one side. "What are you talking about?" he asked.

"This isn't quicksand," Magford explained and did his best to worm out of the sludge. "It's a Roarcaneum, creature of the ground. And we've been caught right in his jaws."

"Try Shadow Tumbling!" Jessicana called out desperately, but Roseabelle shook her head.

"It won't work!"

Magford stared at Jessicana, his eyes wide and determined. "Jessicana, stab your javelin into the ground now! It'll get it to resurface and then you can fight it." Jessicana's pulse was beating rapidly, and she bit her lip.

"So the Darvonians did find us!" Astro said, scrambling to pull himself out.

Jessicana gathered all of her courage and looked all over the ground, holding out her javelin. Where was she supposed to attack the Roarcaneum? She'd read about these creatures in books before but they never specified where to stab them—that was the only way to get rid of them.

"Just do it!" Magford hollered as the sludge buried them shoulder deep. Acting on an impulse, Jessicana lifted up her javelin and drove it deep into the earth. The reaction was instant. The ground's radius around them began to vibrate. Jessicana stood her ground, trying to keep from toppling over, and yanked back on the rod of her javelin, breaking a piece of the shaft off. She pulled her javelin from the deep mud. An enormous shape withdrew from the earth, silver eyes glinting at Jessicana. It had a round head with slick mud dripping from its long neck. It also possessed a bulky nose with tiny nostrils, and its soft brown skin surprisingly camouflaged well into the earth. Roseabelle, Magford, and Astro were embedded in its head.

Then Jessicana saw the most bizarre scene she had ever seen. They were sinking right through the monster's head into its mouth! So that was how the Roarcaneum caught its victims.

Jessicana resisted the urge to squeak, and she took a step back. The Roarcaneum was undoubtedly huge—although it towered ten feet over her, part of its lower body was still submerged in the mud. The Roarcaneum stared at her, almost as if it was wondering if Jessicana was really worth attacking. On a sudden impulse, Jessicana suddenly leaped forward and hurled her javelin at it, but the sharp weapon bounced back against its hard coating of solid rock and soil. She yelped as the javelin came sailing back at her, flying over her head as she ducked.

"Hurry, Jessicana!" Roseabelle shouted, and

Jessicana searched for the monster's weak point. It was protected by the earth, submerged in the earth. Then she saw its silver eyes staring past her.

Of course! The reason the Roarcaneum wasn't attacking her was because it couldn't even see her. Jessicana realized it had horrible vision. Its only weapon was to trap its victims and catch them by surprise. Her intellect took over, and she thought quickly, running all possibilities through her head.

Then it came to her. The Roarcaneum had to have an incredible sense of hearing to sense its prey above ground!

She dug in her pack, and the monster growled a bit as her friends frantically twisted out of the mush, striving to escape. Jessicana yanked out a Flame-hurler and loaded it with ammo. Roseabelle, Astro, and Magford were now neck deep in the slush. "Hold on!" she yelled and pulled the trigger.

Three iron balls of metal, electricity, and fire hurled toward the Roarcaneum, zooming right past it and exploding into a cloud of dark silver ash, raining down on the Darvonian ground. The earth monster, hearing the horrendous noise, jerked around to look. Unfortunately, the movement did nothing to release Jessicana's friends.

Jessicana gritted her teeth. The Roarcaneum, still

startled from the commotion, kept looking all around for the noise. She just had to make more of it. Jessicana banged two swords together, but quickly dropped them. She attached a hook to an arrow, placed it in a bow, aimed, and shot. The hook embedded in the Roarcaneum's shoulder, and she quickly grabbed onto it as the Roarcaneum flailed about.

Grasping the arrow as tight as she could, Jessicana screamed as she was flung about. But seeing her friends above her rapidly sinking into the monster's head, she thought harder. *Think, Jessicana, think.*

Wait a second. I can fly! she thought. With not a moment to waste, Jessicana transformed into a parrot and zoomed up to her friends, wings flapping hurriedly. Astro had started hacking at the mud with his sword but that only resulted in bruising his arms as he tried to yank his weapon out of it. "Awk, use your powers!" Jessicana squawked loudly, and Roseabelle and Astro exchanged panicked glances. Jessicana transformed back into a girl in midflight and landed beside them.

Her friends were now shooting lightning bolts and hitting the Roarcaneum in the head with its own rocks. Magford's body had almost sunk through. Jessicana, keeping light on her feet so she wouldn't join their half-buried state, yanked Magford by his arms out of the mud, using all of her strength. She tried to not focus on the creature's height. She could maybe fly simply down but her friends couldn't.

As the Roarcaneum thrashed about, Astro managed to release himself, burning a hole around himself with his silver-blue lightning. He then turned to Roseabelle, digging her out as fast as he could. "Astro, a little help here," Jessicana groaned as she lifted Magford.

She fought to keep her balance as the Roarcaneum tromped around, following the many noises. She concentrated on not toppling over the edge even though the ground was shaking violently. "Astro, give me your pack!" she yelled over the monster's sudden roaring.

The lightning boy tossed it to her. Jessicana grabbed a Flame-hurler, loaded it up, and set it off. A single ball of ammo hurled toward the creature's eyes.

And then the Flame-hurler exploded in a flash of smoke.

Coughing and sputtering, a dark cloud of fog smothered them and Jessicana could faintly hear the wailings of the creature as it tipped this way and that. "Moonstar!" Magford yelled, but before he could continue, the Roarcaneum tilted drastically, and Jessicana tumbled through the air. Her vision clouded, her senses muddled—and then, suddenly, her limbs felt as though they were on fire.

An excruciating jolt of pain shot through her leg, and Jessicana instantly sat up straight. She was positioned on the back of Moonstar, but she had landed wrong. One of her legs was sticking out at an odd angle. She cringed, her arms shaking.

Roseabelle and Magford appeared beside her, and Astro came plummeting down, flailing wildly. Roseabelle and Astro scrambled over to Moonstar and threw themselves on top of his back

Moonstar instantly sprinted away, and Jessicana clutched his sleek fur. As the Roarcaneum bellowed, Roseabelle, Magford, and Astro were carted across the rough Darvonian terrain, dark clouds blocking the sun.

"Won't it come after us?" Jessicana yelled over the sound of the wind rushing past their faces.

Magford shook his head.

"It's almost impossible to destroy a Roarcaneum, but the fortunate part is that it can't follow us," Magford said. "It's too grounded."

"But it wasn't there last night!" Jessicana heard Astro say, her energy seeping away. She managed to sit up. She was glad she hadn't been required to completely destroy the Roarcaneum. Jessicana hated hurting animals of any kind and only did it in self-defense.

"The Darvonians must have planted it, moved it somehow," Magford shouted back. "They probably were watching us from afar."

Moonstar raced up a dark hill, passing large walls of stones and hidden fortifications. They sped by Darvonian encampments, but they were traveling so quickly, the Darvonians couldn't see them, let alone stop them. Jessicana noticed Magford was staring intently at Moonstar, and she figured they were probably mentally communicating.

She glanced at her leg and winced, gritting her teeth. She hadn't broken it—Jessicana could tell due to her experience as a healer—but it still surged with pain. She gripped Moonstar's fur.

Moonstar suddenly came to a stop, and everyone was thrown off onto a patch of hard earth. Jessicana's leg hit a hard boulder, and she yelped. "Fortunate," she muttered, gritting her teeth as she pulled herself into an upright position. "Really fortunate."

Jessicana's fingers went to her deep tunic pocket where her blue Stone rested. She also took out some water from her pack. Her heart sank when she realized that most of the items inside had fallen out. But she still had her javelin and some leftover ammo from the Flame-Hurler. A needle-like pain shot through her leg again, and she dug through her tunic pockets as her face twisted in a grimace. Where was her potion kit?

Jessicana caught hold of a tiny metal container and pulled it out to see her emergency potion kit. Of course, it wasn't her full collection of potions and herbs so she couldn't heal fully, but at least the kit would fix her leg a little bit. She dipped her finger into some gray paste and swallowed it, shivering at the grainy taste. That should do it.

Magford helped Roseabelle up, and then Jessicana who gladly accepted his hand. Astro popped to his feet. They were standing on a rocky tall hill, and Magford nodded firmly. "Listen closely, very closely. Astro and Jessicana, you must take out your Stones and press them together. Their power will attract Roseabelle's Stone." He took a deep breath. "Meanwhile, I'm going to distract the Darvonians."

"What?" Roseabelle burst out, rushing to her father's side. Jessicana and Astro exchanged worried looks. Magford couldn't go into the midst of Darvonians—he could be caught again! He bent down on his knees to face Roseabelle and smiled gently at her.

"Roseabelle, from what you've told me, you've grown into an amazing person. You're an intelligent, brave girl, and I'm proud to call you my daughter. Once you obtain the Stones, follow Moonstar—he knows where the physical entrance to the Dream World is.

"You have to go inside, with your friends or alone, and go to the very core of the Dream World, avoiding Darvonians, creatures, whatever else may be there."

Roseabelle shook her head. "You already disappeared once. I'm not letting that happen again!"

Magford took her by the shoulders. "It won't. I'll come back, I promise. Dastrock and Danette should be fine, as well. I'll find them if I can. Be safe, be careful." Before they could stop him, he drew his double swords, offered them a half smile, and ducked into the shadow of the hill, closing his eyes and instantly vanishing. In a matter of seconds, he had Shadow Tumbled away without a trace.

"No!" Roseabelle exclaimed, and Jessicana touched her arm, smiling reassuringly at her friend.

"Come on," she said. "You can do this. Get the Third Eye. We don't know how the Stone is going to come to us."

Astro yanked the Stone out of his pocket and tossed Roseabelle the spyglass. She caught it in one hand and raised it to her eye. Jessicana cautiously withdrew her Stone and held it up to Astro's. The two glimmering surfaces pushed against each other.

For a moment, nothing happened. Jessicana shifted a bit. "See anything?" she asked Roseabelle, but her friend shook her head.

"No," Roseabelle muttered. Minutes droned on with Jessicana and Astro's Stones still pressed together.

Astro was about to open his mouth to suggest a new idea when Roseabelle suddenly perked up. "Guys . . . I see something . . ."

Jessicana grinned but it quickly faltered. The hill had begun to quake.

CHAPTER 13

The Chase

AS THE GROUND BENEATH HIM SHOOK VIO-
lently, Astro gripped his gleaming red gem.
Gusts of air blew at the trio, and Astro
squinted his eyes. Everyone's hair was tossed about
in the wind. Out of the corner of his eye, he spotted
Jessicana's tiny potion kit and most of their weapons
fly away. He could see Roseabelle standing her ground
as she clutched the Third Eye tightly in her hands.

Digging his feet into the soil, he raised a hand up
to protect himself when suddenly it all stopped, and
an eerie hush fell over the hills. Astro searched the
landscape, and his eyes brightened when he saw a glittering object zooming toward them.

He glanced at his and Jessicana's Stones, the blue and red, and then back to Roseabelle's healing Stone flying quickly at them. He hurriedly caught it in one hand and gave it to Roseabelle.

"Why was there so much wind?" Jessicana asked.

"I'm guessing it was buried in the ocean floor," Roseabelle said. "Maybe the gravitational pull of the two Stones was so much it had to burrow itself out of there."

Moonstar had taken cover below the hill and climbed up to meet them. Astro noticed that Jessicana's backpack had flown away, but luckily she still had her ammo, javelin, and, of course, her Stone. His pack had been lightly positioned on his back and still remained there. Roseabelle had managed to grasp onto the Third Eye.

"Come on," Jessicana urged. The girls mounted Moonstar, and Astro was about to follow when a silver jagged disc sped past his head, barely nicking his ear. A Thepgile! He jumped in surprise and whirled around, protectively raising his hands in front of him.

"Astro," Roseabelle whispered. "Look."

He scrutinized the landscape closer and saw dark shadowy figures perched in trees and hiding below the hill. Darvonians.

There had to be hundreds of them, all armed with weapons. How could they have not seen them before?

Astro shot a range of high-powered bolts at the line of the Darvonians. He mounted Moonstar when arrows flew past his head. Jessicana and Roseabelle had already jumped onto Moonstar.

"GO!" he yelled, and the Sheilvoh took off running, speeding past the throngs of waiting Darvonians. It was extremely lucky that the trio had Moonstar on their side. Astro figured that animals on Metamordia had powers as well, not only amazing speed but also incredible strength.

Jessicana glanced behind them. "They're not far behind!"

"It's all right. Don't look back, just focus on the horizon!" Roseabelle shouted back.

Ignoring her, Astro turned to see the Darvonians—but they weren't alone. His fingertips tingled when he saw the dark shadowy shapes they rode.

Shadow Horses.

Astro reasoned that the Shadow Horses had come from Metamordia but had been tainted by Darvonians so they could ride them. He clenched his teeth and held out his hands toward them. Enormous lightning bolts erupted from out of his fingertips.

Sure enough, pain flashed through his hands, and he tightly curled them into fists. "Astro—" Jessicana started to say.

"It's all right! I've got it," he cut her off. He wanted to reassure her, but Astro knew he probably wouldn't be able to shoot another round of lightning. The Shadow Horses radiate too much electricity, which overloaded him when he shot lightning. It also caused immense pain. Astro had finally resolved something. If the Shadow Horses were Darvonian, they would've known a long time ago. They had to have come from Metamordia.

Moonstar darted past rocky ledges and tall villages, bounding and leaping skillfully across the landscape. Astro, in the very back, nearly fell off twice. The Darvonians were still riding after them, but quite a few of them had stopped, which made Astro feel a little uneasy. What were they doing? He knew that the Darvonians wouldn't just give up. Up ahead, he heard Roseabelle mutter something. "What?" he yelled, his voice catching in his throat.

"Moonstar's taking us to Kinetle's castle!" Roseabelle shouted back. Astro saw that she was right. Kinetle was the ruler of Darvonia, Sheklyth's mother.

He felt the Sheilvoh's muscles tense a bit more, his pace gradually slowing. "Moonstar's getting tired!" he yelled. "He probably can't carry us much longer."

"I've got it covered!" Jessicana shouted. "I'll transform and follow you as best as I can." Without another word, she jumped into the air, transforming into a parrot midflight and soared above them. Although Moonstar was too quick for her, Astro could still keep sight of the tiny colorful dot in the sky that was Jessicana.

Moonstar traveled through the marketplace in a wild frenzy, knocking over carts and stands. Astro recognized it as the Darvonian courtyard marketplace they had come to while trying to find Danette, not too long ago.

"Is the door in the castle?" he shouted to Roseabelle.

"I'm not sure!" she responded. Moonstar swerved in the dark cobblestone path streets, leaping over surprised Darvonians. Astro tried to focus on their surroundings but everything became a blur as Moonstar gave an extra burst of speed. He thought he saw the enormous structure of the dark castle fly past him, but he wasn't sure. The next thing he knew, he was staring up at the foggy sky. He could hear Roseabelle groaning beside him, and Astro rubbed his head as a headache pounded into his skull. Beside them, Moonstar was lying on his belly, paws out in front.

Jessicana suddenly landed beside them and turned back into a girl. She wiped away the sweat from her forehead. "That . . ." she panted. "Was the most exhausting flight ever."

Astro wanted nothing more than to take a long

nap. All the air was knocked out of him. He struggled to his feet. A silver jagged disc came swinging at him and he dodged it, the blade nicking his ankle, leaving a shallow cut. He looked back at the marketplace courtyard and saw cloaked Darvonians mounted on their Shadow Horses, cantering toward them. A few Darvonians had already drawn their weapons.

Roseabelle got to her feet, looking a bit woozy as well. "Come on," she said. "We have to get to the door, wherever it is." She put a hand on Moonstar's lithe form, and the Sheilvoh rose to its full extent. "Come on, Moonstar," she whispered in the animal's ears.

Moonstar seemed to sense the urgency of her tone. The Sheilvoh set off at a normal pace, and the three friends stumbled after Moonstar, who circled the vast perimeter of the castle. Behind them, the furious thundering of hooves followed. "They're gaining on us!" Astro shouted. He clutched his bloodred Stone, thinking how much easier it would be if the Stones worked in Darvonia.

Just then, a group of Shadow Horses, Darvonians mounted proudly on top, veered straight in front of them, blocking their path. Astro stopped in his tracks as the Darvonians pointed their weapons at them.

They were completely surrounded. Again.

CHAPTER 14
The Invisible Door

ROSEABELLE LET OUT A GASP WHEN THE DARvonians jumped out in front of them. Another group blocked their escape from behind. The Darvonians circled around them, enclosing the three friends and Moonstar.

Moonstar bounded back to the trio, stepping in front of them and growling. He purred softly, rubbing against Roseabelle's leg and nuzzling his horn against her pocket. What was he doing? She placed her hand inside, her fingers closing around the Stone and then the small spyglass. She carefully brought out the Third Eye. Maybe the Sheilvoh wanted to tell her something about it.

She put a hand on his head, then felt a rush of urgency directed at the spyglass. Discreetly, Roseabelle put the spyglass to her eye.

Something caught her vision—a brown object in the distance, floating in the air. A thrill ran through Roseabelle. Of course! It had to be the door to the Dream World, hidden by an enchantment to keep it invisible.

Roseabelle removed the spyglass from her face and stuffed it in her pocket before the Darvonians could notice it. She then peered past their enemies, seeing a cluster of jutting rocky stones from the path. Focusing intently on them, her mind lifted the boulders into the air behind the Darvonians.

Soft gentle breezes sifted through the area. The Darvonian in the front dismounted. "Where are the Stones?" the Darvonian asked, deathly quiet. Roseabelle recognized the voice—it was Heltonine, Sheklyth's younger sister! Heltonine turned to Astro. "It wouldn't be wise to shoot your lightning at us now." Roseabelle understood what she was saying. They were surrounded by so many Shadow Horses that the overpowering rush of power inside Astro could seriously injure him.

Concentrating hard on the boulders, Roseabelle used her telekinesis to lift them and lead them over to

Heltonine. She felt Jessicana tense beside her. Roseabelle tried to block out all other thoughts from her mind as Heltonine carefully approached them.

"Fly," Astro whispered to Jessicana.

Roseabelle barely heard Jessicana's reply. "I'm not leaving you guys."

Roseabelle surreptitiously watched the boulders she was sneakily positioning above the Darvonians. Heltonine stopped a few paces in front of them, looking puzzled that the three friends weren't reacting to what she was saying. All was quiet as she surveyed the trio.

Suddenly Roseabelle tilted her head. The cluster of boulders hovering over the Darvonian's heads dropped, knocking the Darvonians to the ground. They remained motionless. Commotion instantly filled the courtyard. Jessicana quickly shot into the air as a parrot, but not before tossing Roseabelle her javelin and Astro some Flame-Hurler ammo. Roseabelle guessed Jessicana had quietly rummaged through her pack.

Because Roseabelle had kept the boulders behind the Darvonians before raising and dropping them from above, the Darvonians from behind hadn't seen anything at all. But now the Darvonians instantly reacted, and a dozen arrows rained down on Roseabelle and Astro. Roseabelle quickly side-stepped a cluster of arrows and swung her javelin to bat another away. Two others whistled past her ankles, and Astro quickly hurled some ammo at the group, which exploded into a mixture of dark fog, fire, and ash. A foggy wall rose up between Astro and the Darvonians. Roseabelle could hear Darvonians coughing and spluttering on the other side. "Come on!" she said, and Astro and she sprinted away from the throngs of Darvonians. Moonstar followed close behind, skillfully dodging all the missiles thrown at them.

Jessicana was already a few yards ahead. "Where's the door?"

"I saw it with the spyglass!" Roseabelle exclaimed, but Moonstar had already bounded ahead, leading them to it.

"Hurry!" Jessicana said.

"I think reinforcements are coming," Astro said, pointing upward. Darvonians had appeared on the buildings' balconies and towers. The sky began raining weapons. Roseabelle eyed the Dream World door and inside her pocket, her Stone began to vibrate.

"Do you feel that?" she asked, her eyes lighting up. "Of course! The Stones are regaining their power since they're so close to the Dream World's entrance!" They continued sprinting, thrilled at the sudden sizzle of energy in their pockets.

Suddenly a slew of arrows shattered the air around them. Roseabelle looked to see Darvonian archers shooting from the castle—the fog had cleared up and the enemy had spotted them. An arrow nearly hit Jessicana's leg, and Roseabelle felt one of the arrows nick her shoulder.

She saw they had two balls of ammo left, which Astro was holding. "Wait for it," he muttered as all three of them sprinted.

"Uh, Astro, I think you should throw that right about now!" Roseabelle's voice had a nervous edge to it as a Thepgile snapped at them. She quickly jumped out of the way as its owner reeled it back. They were running as fast as they could, following in Moonstar's tracks. Reinforcements had come, and Darvonians poured out of the castle at an alarming rate.

"Just a few more seconds," he countered as more Darvonians suddenly burst into view, with bows nocked and swords drawn.

Astro hurled one of the ammo balls at them, and a thick fog sprang up once again. Moonstar suddenly stopped and rubbed against something solid. Roseabelle raised the spyglass to her eyes, and she saw a room floating a few feet above them. Moonstar was rubbing against a pillar in the center that kept the room standing. A white door faced out of one of the room's walls, and she could see the glassy tube coming from it. A brown door led inside in the room.

"Hurry!" Astro shouted.

More arrows rained down from random directions; the Darvonians couldn't see it.

Jessicana flew up as a parrot and landed on a ledge beside the door. "Roseabelle, jump!" she called.

Bending her knees, Roseabelle focused and leaped, falling short by a few inches.

"I'll boost you up," Astro said, and Roseabelle quickly climbed on his shoulders. The smoke was clearing up; they didn't have much time. But as Astro stood up, she toppled over. He groaned. "Really, Roseabelle?"

Jessicana suddenly shook her head. "What am I doing?" she said incredulously. She withdrew her Stone, waved it, and a staircase appeared under their feet.

Moonstar leaped up and Roseabelle and Astro charged up it. Astro vanished the steps with his red Stone once they were safely positioned on the ledge. Jessicana threw open the door and they piled in, Roseabelle quickly closing it behind her.

Finally safe, at least for now, Roseabelle realized

they had plunged into a tiny dark cellar, lit dimly by some torches placed on the wall. Roseabelle reached into her pocket and grabbed the glittering white gem.

"There it is," Roseabelle said, gesturing to the almost transparent door. On it were positioned three scooped openings, one for each Stone.

"Wait," Jessicana said as Roseabelle moved toward it. "Shouldn't one of us stay here? I mean what if the Dream World door closes on us and we're stuck in there forever?"

"Or worse, if Darvonians come down here and enter in while we're gone," Astro added.

"Or even worse, if something in there gets out," Jessicana continued.

"Or—"

Roseabelle laughed and put up a hand to stop them. "All right, I see your point. I'll go in alone." She swallowed, immediately regretting her words. "Once the Stones are in position, I'll quickly Shadow Tumble back to the entrance, so I won't be demolished with the rest of the Dream World."

"Are you sure?" Jessicana asked, coming up beside her friend. Roseabelle hesitated. She didn't know what was waiting for her, and the only thing she was armed with was the trutan and a javelin.

"I have my powers," she said. "I'll be all right." Astro and Jessicana nodded solemnly. "But if anything goes wrong, you have to destroy the Dream World."

"Don't talk like that," Astro said. "You can do this, Roseabelle. We believe in you."

Jessicana leaped forward and hugged her, and Astro gave her a reassuring grin. Roseabelle managed a small smile back. Even Moonstar rubbed affectionately against her leg.

Roseabelle crossed to the door and placed the white Stone inside of the door. "Wait," Roseabelle said and pulled out the trutan. She couldn't exactly do anything with it in the Dream World except lose it. "The Darvonians will come through the door, so use this to create anything you might need. They might've seen us disappear through open air and figured out where this room is."

Astro accepted the parchment. "Thanks, Roseabelle," he said. Together he and Jessicana put their Stones in the door, the gems clicking in place. The door instantly radiated a soft silver-white glow and it gently swung open, a soft mist flowing out of it. Roseabelle tried to peer ahead but all she could see was a glowing passageway. Astro removed the Stones from the door and handed them to her.

To their left, the door abruptly flew open. "Well,

this is fortunate," a silky voice said. A Darvonian emerged from the shadows, followed by two guards dressed in cloaks. Roseabelle scowled. The fog must have cleared; the Darvonians had spotted them entering the room.

"Go, Roseabelle!" Jessicana urged. "Now."

The center Darvonian threw off her hood to reveal a familiar face. Roseabelle gaped. Of course! This Darvonian resembled an older Heltonine. It was Kinetle, ruler of the Darvonians. Roseabelle flinched and took a step backward, toward the open door of the Dream World. Her two friends were alone, cornered in a small room, standing up against three dangerous, fully-armed Darvonians. She couldn't just leave them!

Moonstar emitted a deep growl and sprang at one of the Darvonians. Okay, maybe they weren't so alone. "Roseabelle, go!" Astro shouted.

Roseabelle glanced into the Dream World.

"I can't believe I'm doing this," she whispered to herself and ran through the door to the Dream World. She left the door halfway open. It had to be left open or she wouldn't be able to come back. The last thing she saw was Astro, hurling their last ammo ball at Kinetle, and the room crackling with electricity.

CHAPTER 15

The Dream World

ROSEABELLE TOOK A DEEP BREATH; SHE HOPED her friends would be fine. She looked down the passage of the Dream World. It was eerily quiet but she knew it wasn't empty. Roseabelle took a cautious step forward, amazed by all the mist floating in the air.

A light shone up ahead, and she continued down the tunnel, rounding the corner. An unbelievable sight greeted her eyes.

The landscape was dark and rocky—it mirrored Darvonia exactly, which was kind of scary. It stretched as far as the eye could see, and Roseabelle could even spot where she'd met Ugagush, Sheklyth's brother, for the first time.

When Roseabelle had traveled here in her mind, she had concluded that Darvonians gathered here, because she had seen Kinetle's son here. She had touched Asteran's feather and been instantly transported. She figured that the Darvonians made specific objects so they could meet here. So Darvonians could come here mentally but never physically. Roseabelle scoured the black sandy beach for anyone, but she saw nothing.

Except for . . . Her eyes widened when she noticed some black clad figures in the far distance, huddling in a small group. Those had to be the Darvonians Astro had vanished with his Stone. That meant among them was Sheklyth. The thought made Roseabelle shudder.

So where was the center of the Dream World? Roseabelle searched the sky but saw no clouds. The sky was just plain black, artificial, and unmoving. Roseabelle thought hard back to the conversation with her father about moving through the Dream World as quick as the wind. Was that really possible?

She pictured herself moving through the land as quick as the air. Instantly, an invisible force propelled her forward. Roseabelle's eyes widened and she imagined herself coming to a halt. Her actions obeyed her thoughts. "No way," she murmured, and her hand went to her javelin. There was a rocky black mountain beyond the group of Darvonians. It would make sense if the center of the Dream World was in there, because it was more prominent and large, but the mountain was miles away.

Roseabelle took a deep breath. The Darvonians would probably notice her if she sped by, but she had to hurry! She didn't have much time—Astro and Jessicana were still taking on the Darvonians back in Darvonia.

Imagining herself traveling at the speed of wind, Roseabelle closed her eyes and shot forward, an invisible hand pushing her. Her feet skimmed over the black grainy sand, and Roseabelle realized this place was almost a replica of Darvonia. Except for the looming mountain in the distance.

Her vision sped by in a blur. As Roseabelle shot by the Darvonians, she heard some confused shouts. She neared the mountain, clutching the Stones in her hands. They felt heavy in her tired arms.

Faster, she thought to herself. *Come on. You can do it!*

Glancing over her shoulder, Roseabelle saw distorted black figures chasing after her. Maybe they hadn't seen who she was but they probably were curious. She had to destroy the Dream World before they could get the Stones.

The Darvonians were traveling at the speed of

wind also. Roseabelle saw the blurred figures following her, and she gritted her teeth, putting all her strength into reaching that mountain. She closed her eyes, thinking of Astro and Jessicana, her mother and father, and Benotripia. She had to get there in time!

She suddenly halted in her tracks, the force nearly toppling her over. She was already halfway up the mountain. Roseabelle spotted a boulder and ducked behind it just as the Darvonians shot right past. She counted two seconds and then once again emerged, speeding across the ascending black stone.

Her breath whipped out of her throat, Roseabelle peered up ahead to see the Darvonians slowing down, probably wondering where she had disappeared to—and then she passed them. She focused on holding onto the Stones and her only weapon.

Roseabelle focused on the mountain's peak and her face split into a wide grin. This was it. Benotripia was finally going to have peace! The solution was just moments away!

But a hard hand suddenly gripped her wrist. The combination of her intense speed and the abrupt pull on her arm caused Roseabelle to fling backward onto the hard ground. The javelin landed to her right and the Stones scattered all over the ground.

She instantly jumped to her feet, seizing the

javelin and the blue and white Stones, but a pale hand grabbed the red Stone before she could reach it. Roseabelle looked up to see the group of Darvonians right before her, armed with shields, swords, maces, and other kinds of equipment. *Why did Astro have to make them disappear with their weapons?* she thought.

Her blood went ice cold when she saw who was at the front. A smirk was on her face and the red Stone in her hand.

Sheklyth, a black cloak encircling her, looked no different from the day she had betrayed the Benotripians.

Roseabelle immediately leaped forward with her javelin, swinging at Sheklyth's hands and taking the Darvonian by surprise—she obviously hadn't been expecting Roseabelle to attack her. The red Stone fell from Sheklyth's grip, and Roseabelle dived forward.

As she lunged for the Stone, Roseabelle suddenly found the tip of a sword at her throat. She backed away, realizing that one of the Darvonians had caught the Stone. Sheklyth snatched it from him hurriedly.

"How did you even find out about this place?" Sheklyth asked, her intense eyes staring into Roseabelle's. Roseabelle had faced Sheklyth many times before—as a friend, as a new foe, and now as an old enemy. Sheklyth had been her former trainer going by the name of Shelby, pretending to be a Benotripian while actually spying for Darvonia.

"Give me the Stone," Roseabelle said slowly, readying her javelin. She didn't know what else to do or say; the Darvonians definitely outnumbered her. Up ahead, she could see the peak of the mountain. There was some sort of silvery basin—that was where she needed to go. She just had to get that Stone . . .

Sheklyth reached inside of her cloak. "You're too late, you know. The Darvonians are already here."

"What?" Roseabelle asked, her thoughts turning furiously. What was her former trainer talking about? Just then, Sheklyth took the opportunity to strike with a long dagger. Roseabelle quickly blocked the blow with her javelin. The other Darvonians attempted to approach them, but Sheklyth just handed the red Stone to them, most likely making sure she wouldn't lose it in battle.

Roseabelle drove the hilt of her javelin at Sheklyth, but the Darvonian sliced through it with her dagger, cutting Roseabelle's weapon in half. Sheklyth took another jab at her, and Roseabelle stumbled a bit but managed to sidestep it. "Face it, Roseabelle. You're beat."

Seeing her broken weapon, Roseabelle glanced at the Stones in her hand. Should she use them to conjure another weapon for herself? Roseabelle could only create, not summon objects with the blue Stone; otherwise, she would've have tried to get the red Stone from out of the Darvonian's grasp.

Deciding against it, Roseabelle dashed to the side, ducking into the shadow of a large boulder. Before the Darvonians could reach her, she pictured a spot right behind the Darvonians and stomped her foot.

Instantly, Roseabelle appeared right behind Sheklyth, literally in her shadow. She wrenched the Stone from the Darvonian's grip, thwacking Sheklyth's fists with the pole of her broken javelin. As Sheklyth cried out in pain, Roseabelle darted up the mountain. She could hear heavy footsteps behind her and turned back partway, focusing on a particular patch of hard gritty earth. As the Darvonians advanced, she backed up the mountain, levitating a loose chunk of dry earth. She moved her head to the side and it splattered down on the Darvonians, knocking them to the ground.

Roseabelle raced to the top of the mountain and realized it wasn't a basin she had been looking at. Instead, it was an embellished silver bowl perched on top of a staff. This had to be it. Nothing else in the Dream World had beckoned to her like this object did.

She was about to place all three Stones in the bowl when a black arrow pierced her sleeve, slamming her arm against the bowl. Two of the Stones slipped from her hand and tumbled from view. Roseabelle glanced over her shoulder to see hundreds of Darvonians pouring from the passage into the Dream World, all armed with weapons. Fear penetrated her mind, fuzzing up her senses, and Roseabelle did her best to push it away. She was too close now to give up! There were hundreds of Darvonians, it seemed. Roseabelle wouldn't be surprised if they were streaming from every corner of the island.

Black-clad figures were zooming up the mountain. Roseabelle hurriedly slammed the red Stone into the bowl and watched as the silver melded around it. The gem had become part of the bowl. She bent down and stretched out her uninjured arm for the other two glittering jewels that lay innocently on the black sand. She grabbed the blue Stone and soon it was melded into the bowl as well.

One more.

Adrenaline pumping and heart racing, she reached for the third Stone. Suddenly, a piercing pain engulfed her leg. She thudded to the ground over the white Stone, face twisted in agony.

An arrow had struck her leg. Breathing heavily, she saw that the Darvonians were filling the entire top of the mountain. As one group surrounded her, another walked over to inspect the bowl.

Agony like she had never felt before racked Roseabelle's body, racing up and down her limbs in hot flashes of pain. She knew she had to get the last Stone. Where was it? She was too stricken, too paralyzed with stabbing pain to move. A part of her knew it was all over. The Darvonians had entered the Dream World and it had not been destroyed. All her friends' adventures and sacrifices had been in vain.

But as she stared vacantly at the ground, Roseabelle pictured her friends at the entrance, waiting for her to return, fighting just so she could succeed. Jessicana and Astro had always been there for her—she couldn't just abandon them now! Benotripia would be overrun if she did nothing. But what could she do? She was surrounded. Sheklyth had won.

Tears pooled in her eyes as Roseabelle recalled one more thing—she had finally found her father. If she survived the Dream World, her family would be united once again. The joyful faces of Danette, Dastrock, and Magford, all together—that was all she had wished for her entire life.

Roseabelle wanted to see her father again, wanted to tell him how glad she was to find him at last. She wanted to see her mother's face when she saw Magford. All the things she wanted now seemed distant, like a dream.

Here she was lying on the ground, helpless, wounded. But thinking about her friends and her family filled her with sudden warmth. Hope. It fueled her. It wasn't over yet. There was still time.

She'd been in dangerous situations before. Roseabelle knew she had to figure something out before the Darvonians found the other Stone and whisked it away.

Roseabelle heard the Darvonians trying to remove the Stones from the bowl, but it didn't work. Sheklyth's sharp voice struck her ears. "What's done is done, but the Dream World is still standing. Get the girl out of here! Is she dead yet?"

"Probably just in too much pain to move," a gruff voice responded.

Roseabelle's thoughts raced through her mind, and she shifted a bit. An arrow to the upper leg could be fatal if it wasn't treated right away. She could see the black arrow protruding from her, and the pain was growing more intense.

Out of the corner of her eye, Roseabelle spotted a gleaming object right near her foot. It was her Stone, radiating as clear as the noonday sun. If only she could get a bit closer to it. Gritting her teeth, Roseabelle shifted back a bit and ignored the pain.

She grunted. Her breathing became more shallow as she inched toward it and covered it with her feet.

"Retrieve the white Stone! Where is it?" Sheklyth hissed from above. Roseabelle forced herself not to panic.

Gathering every last ounce of strength she had, Roseabelle focused on the Stone, and it suddenly scooted over to her, settling beside her wounded leg.

She could feel it right under her leg, healing her. She heard the Darvonians scuttling around to find the Stone and knew that this was the opportune moment to strike.

Roseabelle sat up with a start, wrenched the arrow from her leg, grabbed the Stone, and quickly plunged it into the bowl before anyone had a chance to react. The silver instantly melded around it, and the ground began to shake.

"No!" Sheklyth shrieked. "Retreat! Retreat!" She lunged for Roseabelle, her eyes mad with fury. Roseabelle dodged her, ducking into the silver bowl's shadow. Trembling, Roseabelle pictured the shadow of the Dream World doorway.

Her body felt as though it were folding this time as she Shadow Tumbled. Roseabelle knew the Dream World was about to collapse on top of them. She was jolted back to the present as she appeared in the foggy passage with the door to the Dream World on her left. She had to get out before it was too late!

CHAPTER 16

Vanquished at Last

ASTRO AND JESSICANA WERE STANDING IN the doorway, eyes wide. "Roseabelle!" Jessicana yelled and ran forward, grabbing her friend's arm and pulling her to safety. Astro then slammed the door firmly behind them.

Roseabelle toppled onto the floor, body weak with exhaustion, her mind still woozy from using the Dream World to travel so fast. How did her father do that all the time?

"Roseabelle!" Astro said, grinning wildly. "You did it!"

"We were about to come in after you," Jessicana said seriously. "Suddenly all these Darvonians appeared and we did our best to stop them but they pushed right past us. They were too greedy in pursuit of the Dream World. There were too many of them, there was nothing we could do!"

Roseabelle laughed and hugged both of her friends at the same time. "It doesn't matter. You guys were waiting for me! That's what matters!"

They heard a deep shuddering sound at the other end of the room, and the three friends looked over to see the Dream World's door slowly disappearing. It changed into a semi-solid state and vaporized into mist. "It's gone," Jessicana said softly. Astro let out a whoop.

Soon of all of them were jumping up and down in their excitement—the Darvonians had been vanquished!

"Where's Moonstar?" Roseabelle suddenly asked, her eyes wide.

"I don't know!" Astro said. The Sheilvoh had stayed behind with Jessicana and Astro, but now was nowhere to be found.

"Roseabelle!" called a voice from outside. The stone muffled the sound and it was hard to make out who the voice belonged to.

Astro walked forward, staring at the stone wall. "Who is that?"

"Be careful. It could be a trap," Jessicana insisted.

"Hold on. It sounds like . . . my father!" Roseabelle said, grinning broadly.

"I'll blast through it," Astro said, striding up to the wall.

"But what about the Shadow Horses, Astro?" Jessicana inquired.

"I'm pretty sure they're gone," Astro said. "I don't feel overloaded with electricity or anything." He stretched forth his fingers and shot a range of lightning at the wall, peppering it with bolts. Jessicana and Roseabelle both took cover by dropping to the floor as lightning flashed across the room. It looked like Astro was engulfed in a radiating dome of silver and blue. Suddenly there was a white flash. Roseabelle shut her eyes, hiding them from the searing pain.

Jessicana tapped her on the shoulder and Roseabelle slowly opened her eyes to see a smoking crater in the wall and Astro standing beside it. He grinned and rubbed his hands together. "And that's how you do it, folks."

Jessicana coughed on the dust that was rising from the leftover debris. She rolled her eyes and stepped forward, picking her way through the broken slabs of stone. "And you said you weren't overloaded with electricity." Astro grinned sheepishly.

Roseabelle stood up and then stopped short in her

tracks; on the other side of the hole in the wall stood three figures smiling at her. "Mom! Dad! Dastrock!" Roseabelle ran toward them, hugging her parents. She nearly plowed them over. She spotted Moonstar crouched beside Magford.

Danette immediately reached down to embrace her. "Darling, did you really—?"

Magford, who had stepped inside, nodded and grinned broadly. "She did." He shook his head. "Roseabelle, how did you do it? You took on hundreds of Darvonians!"

She smiled modestly. "Not really. I just put the Stones in a bowl. If Jessicana and Astro weren't here, I wouldn't have survived." She gestured at her friends and looked up at Dastrock. "I don't understand. What happened to you guys?"

Dastrock smiled. "Remember my power of making illusions? Well, once I received your mottel, which saved all of our lives, I made it look as though our ship was heading in a different direction. Then once we reached land, we abandoned ship and travelled to the Darvonian palace and saw Magford fighting some Darvonians so we joined in to help. The Sheilvoh led us here."

Magford thumped Dastrock on the back and Danette smiled at her husband, pulling him close in an embrace. "What about the Darvonians?" Jessicana asked.

Danette smiled. "Their leaders are now gone. Sheklyth, Heltonine, Kinetle—they were all overcome with the prospect of power, so they went into the Dream World. In fact, there are scarcely any Darvonians left. We have nothing to fear." Roseabelle glanced up to some debris in the air, a trail of where the Dream World had been.

Roseabelle felt all the worry, all the anxiety, and all of bad dreams about Sheklyth simply lift away, and she grinned at her friends. "Well, you know what this means right?"

"Let's go home," Jessicana said.

"And party!" Astro added.

All of them were so fatigued, so weary, that they burst out laughing. Right then and there, they plopped down on the ground, and Jessicana handed Roseabelle the parchment. Astro drew a rather sloppy meal on the trutan, and soon they were eating cheerfully and talking.

"Wait a second," Roseabelle said, turning to Magford. "How come Metamordia was so deserted?"

Magford sighed. "The Darvonians imprisoned all the people. They're stuck inside cliffs that dotted the island. As soon as you rescued me though, the Darvonians traveled to Darvonia, leaving the Metamordians unattended. I received word that they have gotten out safely."

"How do you know that though?" Astro questioned.

Magford shrugged. "Benotripia isn't the only island that uses mottels."

Roseabelle suddenly reached inside her pocket. "Oh no!" she said. "The Third Eye is gone! I must have dropped it in the Dream World." She expected Danette and Dastrock to be angry with her, maybe even a bit disappointed, but Danette just laughed and put an arm around her.

"Roseabelle, you are worth more than the most powerful magical relic in all of the three islands," she said.

Roseabelle's dream had come true right before her eyes. For once in her life, her whole family was reunited.

The smile she wore was brighter than a thousand suns. Or Dragocone Rays, for that matter.

Epilogue

ROSEABELLE SAT AT THE KITCHEN TABLE, HER long red hair dangling down her back, partly tied back by a red ribbon. The blue dress she wore paled against her brown eyes, and she uncertainly glanced at the rainbow medal she gripped in her hands. It was the medal she had received for saving her mother; holding it always gave her a little bit of strength. Swallowing her fear, she slid it around her neck, the metal shining with a pearly radiance.

From the other corner of the room, Moonstar purred softly. "What?" she asked him teasingly. "Are you nervous too? I doubt it. I'm standing up in front of all of Benotripia today and being named." Moonstar just stared at her with his large golden eyes.

"He's says you're being a drama queen," said a deep voice from the top of the stairs. Roseabelle looked up to see her father, Magford, wearing a long-sleeved white shirt and black pants made from Awnshneelia spider silk, one of the rarest and softest fabrics in all of Metamordia.

"I am not!" she protested and stifled a smile when Magford raised his eyebrows at her. "All right, maybe a little. But it's for a good reason. Weren't you a little worried too when you were crowned?"

Magford put an arm around her. "You'll do fine, Roseabelle. I'm so proud of you."

Just then, the front door swung open, revealing Astro and Jessicana. The parrot girl was dressed in a formal aqua dress and the lightning boy was in silver-and-black shirt and pants.

"You're going to be crowned!" Jessicana exploded, hugging Roseabelle. "You're going to be the ruler of Benotripia. This is so exciting!"

Roseabelle laughed while Astro grinned from ear to ear, his fingertips crackling with electricity. "Uh, Astro," she said. "Please keep your hands in your pockets. The last time you were in my house, we had some silver fireworks."

He grinned sheepishly and stuffed his hands in his pockets. "This is so cool, Roseabelle!"

Danette poked her head into the room. "You ready, Roseabelle?"

She sighed. "I-I think so."

"You're ready for this," Danette said. "You realize what today is?"

She nodded solemnly and Magford smiled. "Four years ago, this very day was when the Darvonians were vanquished."

Jessicana bounced up and down. "Come on, Roseabelle. You're ready for this!"

Roseabelle gave her friend a small smile. "But I'm not even Benotripian!"

Danette laughed. "Just because you were born in Metamordia doesn't mean you're not a Benotripian. You grew up here. It's all right to have two homes."

Roseabelle sighed. "All right, I guess I'm ready." Jessicana squeezed her hand and Astro grinned at her. All of them exited her home and scaled down the ladder. Roseabelle's eyes nearly popped open at what she saw.

People as far as the eye could see clumped together, some sitting in chairs, some standing, eagerly awaiting her arrival. On the ground there was a glittering red-and-orange stage. Dastrock stood on top of it, holding an intricate scepter out of the same metal that her medal was created from. The rainbow colors glinted brilliantly in the sun.

The Benotripians cheered as Roseabelle descended onto the stage next to Dastrock, her mother and father following. Her friends stood at the left side of the stage, and Astro gave her a big thumbs-up.

Danette regally stood in front of the people as Roseabelle fidgeted behind her. She put on her biggest smile, warmth swelling up in her chest. Maybe she was nervous, but she was more excited. Danette raised her hand and the mumbling chatter instantly vanished. "We gather here today to announce and honor my daughter, Roseabelle, who has gone above and beyond to serve Benotripia. She has bravely battled the Darvonians, defended her friends, and displayed endless courage.

"I am fully aware that the honor of becoming the ruler of Benotripia is normally bestowed to the heir when they are seventeen years of age. But Roseabelle is a different case at fifteen years old. She has given her all to Benotripia. Without her and her friends Jessicana and Astro, we would not be standing here today. Being a ruler is not about receiving; it is about giving. And these past few years, that is exactly what Roseabelle has done. So today, I bestow to her the

Destiny Scepter—" Danette broke her speech as Dastrock held the scepter out in his hands, extending it to her.

Roseabelle looked at her mother and saw her kind face and intelligent eyes. She was smiling warmly, and motioning for her to take the scepter. She saw her father and uncle with identical grins on their faces and Jessicana and Astro, both beaming. Even Moonstar seemed as though he was smiling. Taking a deep breath, she spoke the traditional words: "I accept."

The crowd burst into roaring cheers, and Roseabelle took the scepter and held it in the air. Jessicana and Astro raced to her, embracing her. "That was crazy!" Jessicana said.

"How were you so calm and collected up there?"

"I would have freaked!"

Roseabelle laughed. "Oh, please. Whenever I see you guys out there, I'm completely fine."

And truly and honestly, she was. Because finally, Benotripia was at peace.

Acknowledgments

A T SEVEN YEARS OLD, I WROTE MY VERY first story in a glittery purple notebook and spent an entire summer pouring out my imagination into it. Now, six years later, that story is published, I still have that notebook, and I'm now done with the entire Benotripia series. I can't believe I'm where I am today. Let's just say that I have a lot of people to thank.

Gratitude to my amazing family—Mom, Dad, and Ty for supporting me in everything I do. You guys are truly awe inspiring. The same goes to all three of my grandparents and every single one of my extended family members, especially the ones who dressed up as creepy Darvonians at my second launch party. I couldn't do any of this without you.

Thanks to Rachel Sharp for bringing the

Benotripia characters to life with the out-of-this-world cover art and illustrations.

Also, to my crazy fantastic friends Erin, Samantha, Rianna, Frances, Sarajane, Marina, the three Ashleys, and Emma, for always boosting my morale and making me laugh. Thanks to Annabella, for being the perfect Jessicana.

I want to express deep gratitude to Ms. Kunz who first taught me the basics of writing and to Ms. Pearce for making my middle school experience positive and to Melia, for being so eccentric about my writing.

Jennifer A. Nielsen, Richard Paul Evans, and Frank L. Cole—thank you for being the most inspiring authors and people I've ever met. I'd like to show my appreciation to the Cedar Fort team for being so incredibly wonderful in all they do: Lyle, Angie, Alissa, Kelly, Rodney, and everyone else who has strived to make Benotripia a success.

And last but not least, love to my spectacular readers! Benotripia has been such a blast. Thank you for sharing and enjoying the story. Although the series is complete and I am already missing adventures with Roseabelle, Jessicana, and Astro, I have thoroughly enjoyed writing it. Thank you all for making my dreams a possibility.

Discussion Questions

1. If you could make up your own power, what would it be?

2. If you had the choice to live on one of the three islands—Benotripia, Metamordia, or Darvonia—which would you choose?

3. Roseabelle used her courage to venture into the Dream World, Jessicana used her potions and her wits to escape from the Darvonians, and Astro utilized his lightning to protect himself and his friends. Each of the three friends used their strengths to help each other. What are your strengths? How could you use them to defeat the Darvonians?

4. Why do you think Magford allowed the three friends to go after the Darvonians instead of making them stay behind while he took care of it?

5. What was your favorite part of the book? Why?

6. Do you think a Sheilvoh would make a good companion? Why or why not?

About the Author

McKenzie Wagner is thirteen years old and has adored reading since she was four. Her love of books inspired her to write a book of her own, and she completed the first book of The Magic Wall series, *The Magic Meadow and the Golden Locket*, at age seven and the second book, *The Blue Lagoon and the Magic Coin*, shortly thereafter. With her new series, Benotripia, she has now expanded her writing to appeal to kids of all ages. She wishes to obtain an English degree and continue her path as an author. She currently resides in Utah with her mom, dad, and brother, Ty.